I OWN THIS TOWN

The Mayor Bert Xanadu Xanthology

GERRY FLAHIVE

Published by Modern Story
moviemayor@gmail.com

ISBN: 978-1-7773837-0-1
ISBN (e-book): 978-1-7773837-1-8

Printed in Canada by Rapido Books

Cover design by Trevor Twells
TrevorTwells.com

Cover photo: City of Toronto Archives:
Fonds 1128, Series 381, File 247, Item 10633-8
King Station - April 23, 1953
Photographer: Earnest Edgar Strathy Smith

Back cover photo: City of Toronto Archives:
Fonds 1526, File 44, Item 1

Other images from Creative Commons and public domain sources.

Several articles were originally published by Spacing.ca and Torontoist.com

THE CRITICS ARE TYPING!!

"I am a long-time fan of Bert Xanadu's surreal takes on life. I OWN
THIS TOWN is like Twitter, only heavier! The book is great!"
RICHARD CROUSE, CTV'S *POP LIFE*

"I'm always equal parts fascinated and entertained by the clippings
and quippings of Mayor Bert Xanadu. @MovieMayor makes me
genuinely laugh out loud."
ACTOR & COMEDIAN BRENT BUTT

"As if Groucho Marx had a Twitter feed! Bert Xanadu is reckless,
imaginative, unpredictable — a Canadian unconstrained by his
Canadian-ness. An immensely gifted creation."
ANTHROPOLOGIST & AUTHOR GRANT MCCRACKEN

"@MovieMayor is the most consistently funny thing on the internet
— sublimely brainy and absurd!"
SINGER/SONGWRITER HAWKSLEY WORKMAN

"A laugh-out-loud read that leaves one marvelling at the brain that
produces this comedy gold, seemingly without effort."
OSCAR-NOMINATED FILMMAKER WENDY TILBY

"Gerry Flahive's alter ego Bert Xanadu is the funniest comic act to hit
Toronto since Joan Rivers played Csárda's. A loony but loving send-up
of Toronto that plays with the city's vanity and aspirations with Scud
missile accuracy. Bert Xanadu is to Toronto what Dame Edna is to
snobbery: a satire more accurate than the real thing."
NOVELIST & POET MICHAEL REDHILL

Bert Xanadu is the tops! His vinegary views of life illuminate those
corners we might never know existed, and insane policies we didn't
want to know existed. Toronto's TRUE history.
My favourite book of 1973."
FILM CRITIC ANN BRODIE

To Audrey, Alice, Grace & Finn

CONTENTS

HELPFUL EXPLANATORY PAMPHLET

"Yep — you caught me looking wonderful!"

In I OWN THIS TOWN: THE MAYOR BERT XANADU XANTHOLOGY, Mayor Xanadu, the city's foremost movie showman and sole mayor, presents a sexily official selection from the thousands of municipal missives he issued to his citizens in 1973 (through his state-of-the-art Telex machine, the Thought Lathe), the year some call his most triumphantly expressive and non-linear.

The slim volume, which reminds one of Bert's own slimness circa 1933, also includes several readable essays and typewritten thoughts from the Dominion's own Bürgermeister of Buttered Popcorn (i.e.

Bert) on such serious topics as imperceptible transit delays, the Simcoe St. Goatworks, ersatz product endorsements, streetcar fumigation schedules, steamship arrivals of Hollywood stars like Morey Amsterdam and Shelly Winters, zeppelin sightings, nude projectionists' lawsuits, City Hall laughing gas leaks and just what Raymond Burr is doing in town this week anyway – all the things that make Toronto one of the most recent of world-class cities.

Dash. Panache. Class. Sass. Pulchritude. Cravat. Mere words, but when applied to Bert Xanadu, they exhibit all their meanings, dictionaries be damned. In Bert's short bursts of enthusiasm and slightly longer rage-filled exhortations one can see the inner man, and the city he wears like a heavily-starched tuxedo. We may be the cummerbund, but what a view.

@MovieMayor

FOREWORD BY LORNE GREENE
TELEVISION STAR OF NOTE & FORMER
VOICE OF DOOM

I remember my first encounter with the flamboyant Bert Xanadu as though it were yesterday (perhaps because he dictated much of this to me last night over a late supper of tapioca in his 'thinking office' high atop the Pure Food Building on the Canadian National Exhibition grounds).

We met during production of my 1955 motion picture, *HANDSHAKE FROM HELL* (a sassy time-waster with moxie and a message, or so I'm told), and even though I considered myself a reasonably seasoned actor, I had little exposure to the venal and insatiable packs of Hollywood reporters and gossip traffickers so prevalent in those creamy days. Forty-six of them had burst onto our set during an especially intense belt-buckling scene I was having difficulty with. These craven bloodhounds were after me to corroborate a rumour about my so-called 'tawdry tryst' with some or all of The Lennon Sisters.

Suddenly, as if roused to righteous anger by the arrival of Satan himself, Bert, our picture's amiable publicist, reached into his RCMP goose skin valise and pulled out a Canadian Tire bullwhip with a flourish and an earwax-curdling crack that stopped the tidbit-thirsty mob in their tracks. Surely he wouldn't use this deadly....oh my God, he's now cracking the whip with the intensity of Moses, and with the precision of 1946 world archery champion, the Dane, Einar Tang-Holbeck (I'm citing an archer in this context only because I'm not aware of an equivalent bullwhip champion). Soon enough, fedoras, notebooks and sock garters were flying in all directions, and the terrified pack of press leeches was on the run.

Bert, I later learned, only came to Hollywood to manage press relations whenever he got bored being Mayor of Toronto --- he was a fellow Canadian! We quickly bonded over a shared cup of Bovril (we are both cheap), and I learned of his deep and abiding love of municipal governance, and his perky passion for motion picture exhibition. He's been my only publicist ever since (I think the results speak for themselves), and if I were to create (not that I'm planning to) my own fantastical nude city, Lorne Vegas, in the desert just outside of Reno, I can't think of a better mayor to run it for me!

SEXIER FOREWORD BY MARLENE DIETRICH
CHANTEUSE & MOODY SCHAUSPIELERIN

It's been said many times that I chew men up and spit them out, and while that may be true, Bert Xanadu is unchewable. Oh, lord knows I tried, as we sat, knee to knee, flirting in that peculiar Canadian way (all four knees cannot be touching at any given moment), late into the night after one of my performances at the Royal York's Imperial Room. His eyes flashing with desire and with the queasiness that comes with rheumy eyes, Bert would regale me with tales of lust, sin and expense claims from old Hollywood, even telling me stories involving me and my *RANCHO NOTORIOUS* co-star William 'Fred Mertz' Frawley that, while untrue, were powerfully erotic.

But though Bert's lust-making was more effective than that of any other man in the City of Toronto (or even in the larger Metropolitan Toronto municipality, which encompassed Toronto as well as the boroughs of York, East York, North York, Scarborough and the mysterious Etobicoke), he drew the line at consummation, for he is primarily a leader of men, and only secondarily a lover of women. And so, as dawn would break over the decrepit galoshes factories next to the hotel, Bert would inevitably rise, gulp down the last drops of his raisin nog, kiss my hand, and rush off to thwart yet another City Hall filibuster, as only he could do.

Given my hatred of Toronto, and his pre-oiled toupees, I rarely see Bert these days. But he will always be my Donaudampfschifffahrtselektrizitätenhauptbetriebswerkbauunterbeamtengesell-schaft (a term of endearment in German, its literal meaning is the Association for Subordinate Officials of the Head Office Management of the Danube Steamboat Electrical Services). And I hope he will always be yours too.

MAYOR, MOVIE SHOWMAN,
MAMMOTH TALENT, MAN

City of Toronto Archives, Fonds 1257, Series 1057, Item
1496

Mayor Bert Xanadu is the most. Known as Toronto's Movie Mayor, Bert is the most re-elected mayor in the history of the world (once by a divorce court decree), the most-honoured movie showman (including 2,152 plaques and two spurned knighthoods), the most-quoted Canadian (53,204 international citations in newspapers, greeting cards and wedding speeches, leaving egghead Northrop Frye mumbling in envious disgust), and, some say, the most perfect man, complete and astounding in mind, body, soul and wardrobe. Fiercely proud of Toronto, and smitten with the movies, he leads his city with the kick of a vinegar martini, the drive of a freelance gladiator, the dazzle of a well-lit unicorn and the versatility of a piano-playing minotaur.

He has been elected mayor of Toronto 27 times since the 1930s (due to the city's previous and suspiciously-efficient one-year term of office for municipal politicians) and is the owner and manager of the spanking new Imperial Six, a multiplex palace dedicated solely to physically-entertaining motion pictures, and located smack dab in the middle of Yonge St., the longest street in the world, or perhaps it just feels that long.

He had previously managed, swept and/or owned other motion picture theatres in the city, including the Blink-A-Wee, the Methuselah, the Plotorium, the Splice Mahal, the Rear View Mirror Drive-In, and, of course, the magnificently mouldy Imperial itself, the British Commonwealth's most scrumptious auditorium.

Renowned for his manly approach to civic governance, befriended by insecure Hollywood stars eager to bask in his testosterone-fuelled charm, expert at the arts of threading a 35mm film projector or re-tooling a Soviet popcorn machine, praised for his hypnotically-satisfying public speaking style, and owner of the world's largest collection of snappy comeback lines, Xanadu is the master of the timeless arts of seduction – of both audiences and voters. He has been called "the love child of Cesar Romero and Julius Caesar".

Born in Toronto in 1911 and a graduate of Mt. Pleasant Cemetery High School and the prestigious Kino-Smersh Showmanship Institute of Vladivostok, Russia, Xanadu speaks 12 languages, including Varietyese, and is fond of slim chances and large sandwiches.

Always among the first to embrace new technologies, from Lorne-O-Vision (the only way to correctly exhibit Lorne Greene's skin tone on screen) and, at City Hall, the Lobbyist Dispersal Water Cannon, Bert knows a good thing when he sees one. And when he sees one, he says so, soothingly and scintillatingly.

Typical aimless patrons frozen in contemplation outside the city's most satisfying cinema. (City of Toronto Archives: Fonds 1526, File 44, Item 1)

POLICE CALLED TO SCENE OF INTERMINABLE ANECDOTE

"Look this way? Of course!"

Butter used on Imperial Six popcorn is made from milk from cows that have been shown Bing Crosby films, to ensure smoothness.

The delay at Rosedale subway station due to a high sense of entitlement has now cleared.

. . .

Ornery characters assembling at City Hall to grouse and fulminate are advised to disperse immediately or face castigation and reprobation.

Fun Fact: galvanizing, Martinizing and caramelizing were all invented at the same terrifying meal by a Toronto short order cook on Spadina Avenue in 1948.

Toronto leads the world in the production of shirt cardboard, Halloween operas, husband glue, budgie warmers and religious glitter.

Sad day, as the five giant pewter robots I bought at the 1939 New York World's Fair to guard the City's hydro plants are now thoroughly rusted.

We've run out of road salt, switching to chicken pot pie crusts.

Road conditions: Yonge: hopeless; Bay: pointless; Bathurst: salt-free; Spadina: moot; Dufferin: irrelevant; Bayview: intriguing.

Glamour-puss celebrity Zsa Zsa Gabor in town to unveil her new line of perfume, 'Bait 'n Switch' by Fabergé, now available at Sayvette's.

In addition to fluoride, Toronto tap water contains salt-peter, aftershave, aspirin and cinnamon. On purpose, I mean.

Looking forward to CFTO-TV's hard-hitting new Bruno Gerussi series *TOUPÉE COP*, shot in the parkettes and gravy boat stores of Toronto.

Night falls in Toronto, and with it the pants of a new generation.

. . .

Toronto Transit Commission studies show that most rocky marriages break up before reaching Dundas station.

I have re-asserted the City's control of the designation of Toronto restaurants' 'Soup of the Day'. Tomorrow's is Impertinent Potato.

I bid farewell to our 926 trucks heading for the ghastly Slushfields of Oshawa, there to drain their hellish cargo. Godspeed and gesundheit!

Delay on TTC Yonge line due to the use of 'third rail' as a metaphor has now cleared.

City regulations require that, prior to neutering pets, dogs be given a stiff drink and an explanation; cats just need you to look away.

City axe-grinders union is struggling to find the right metaphor for their grievance with the axe-grinding industry.

No way diarrhea is going to keep Don Chimney out of the Olympic marathon. That's why they call him *BLEACHED LIGHTNING*, now at the Imperial Six.

Police raid toupée factory in Willowdale's notorious chimpanzee district. You do the math.

Opening today at the Imperial Six: a leaky pancreas and an insolvent donkey farm aren't going to keep Raymond Burr from *THE POPE'S ECLAIR*.

. . .

If you spit on a sidewalk in my city, I'll have it suctioned up, atomized and then sprayed on the graves of your ancestors.

Expect delays on the TTC King streetcar today as it is weighed down with decades of expectations.

Police called to scene of interminable anecdote.

Wildcat strike at Simcoe St. Goatworks! Pampered union workers refuse diversification of the company's product line to add wildcat-derived shoe polish.

I love to stand at the back of the cinema, staring at the bald and coiffed heads, as they stare at the screen. They don't know a reel change is imminent.

Nine Imperial Six ushers were injured in a brawl with supercilious studio accountants at the midnight showing of Peter Lawford's blood-taining *PULVERIZE*. I'm so proud!

Imperial Six boasts the world's longest-serving projectionist, Percy Davisville, on site here since 1920, first as a vaudeville dentist. He dozes off when Eddie Albert's on-screen, but then don't we all.

Threadneedle's Murky Water Aquarium on Dufferin St. will be closed today for the monthly consoling of the cuttlefish.

Royal Ontario Museum scientists tell me, though I didn't ask, that dinosaurs lived in Toronto trillions of years ago, lumbering around its unpaved streets, but one couldn't call that living.

· · ·

City Hall's Wedding Chapel is now offering half-weddings, marriages of convenience, prefab oaths, annulment workshops, and marriages made in heaven.

Fun Fact: our park benches are positioned to face away from the sun, in order to reduce sunburns and vanity.

TTC passengers are kindly asked to give up.

Merton St. Industrial Parketeria is now home to the world's largest assembly of placebo factories, manufacturing deceptively ersatz substitutes for aspirin, testosterone, chocolate, detective stories and codpieces. Even one of the buildings is fake!

Tonite on *MANNIX*: Joe says the word 'scrotum' and the place empties out.

City of Toronto goatee census is taking too long to complete, as many men obscure their tiny beardlettes with their hand when ruminating.

As owner and operator of the city's finest cinema, the Imperial Six, I feel every motion picture should be as interesting to a moviegoer as a urine-soaked fire hydrant is to a dog.

Ticketed and towed today: Mrs. Eeeni Mosport's 1961 Ford Spatula, parked inside the lobby of Massey Hall; Mr. Norman Tamblyn's 1970 Fiat Arrivederci, idling with lewd connotations; a delivery moped from Tip Top Tailors, spewing corduroy fumes.

A moment of silence today at noon to mark the passing of mimic Rich Little's impersonation of Herbert Hoover, which no one 'gets' anymore.

· · ·

Rakish but mousy Bud Cort in town to shoot a TV commercial for Eaton's. Apparently they've got a surplus of ironing board covers.

TTC train full of sleeping commuters shunted off to a siding at Davisville station, where Sayvette coffee and cinnamon bear claws await them.

Road salt stains have now spread from my shoes to my pant cuffs to my heart.

My pal Peter Lawford's in town taping his Valentine's Day TV special *LOVE ME, RUB ME, SATIATE ME* with guest star Walter Cronkite.

Fun Fact: the pipe organ at the Flying Buttress Church of the Tumescent Bishopric of Coxwell is what Mrs. Xanadu used to call me when we were first courting.

Love can be sticky. Love can be deceptive. Love can suddenly shift, revealing mottled skin. None of that matters to widowed dandruff cream magnate Liza Minelli, who just wants a *MAIL-ORDER TOUPÉE HUSBAND*. Opening Friday at the Imperial Six.

In Victorian Toronto, to vary their monotonous diet of chaff and hide, people would toss a few pages from a Flemish thesaurus into the pot.

City of Toronto Zeppelin Workers' Winter Helium Camp on Hanlan's Point closed until further notice due to an outbreak of non-organic flatulence.

I'm shuttering the Imperial Six this week as Hollywood's latest crop of pictures fails to rise to a standard of lust induction that our customers expect. Also, three of them star Jim Backus.

. . .

Sad day as Toronto's only all-Morse Code radio station, CDDD-AM, goes off the air tonight at midnight, a victim of the younger generation's perverse obsession with spoken language.

Another morn, and Toronto lurches back to life: the Satanic handkerchief mills on Pape roar to spew their monogrammed spoor; a chestnut cart owner marks his 17th year of no one ever buying; the Eaton Bros. fire their 400th Santa; a giant tarpaulin is tossed atop Centre Island.

A clod with measles. A sultry divorcee with a retractable cigarette shelf. A defrosted podiatrist allergic to lint. These are some of the people who might be sitting next you at the Imperial Six at Peter Lawford's new plot-lite actioner *THE SALAMANDER INVECTIVE*, opening today.

Fun Fact: the Bloor Viaduct was originally meant to be only that: a viaduct, to carry water to the parched of the Danforth, who had never tasted lemonade, or been able to start a viable aquarium business.

Enjoying bazooka-size eclairs as we celebrate the opening of the police department's Alibi Office, world's greatest repository of phony excuses.

To be sure my pants don't fall down I rely on Preenhammer's Suspenders of Disbelief©. They maintain the fiction that your waist is under control!

Tonite on *BARNABY JONES*: a trail of blood, gold coins, Cheetos, hamsters and venetian blinds lead Barnaby precisely nowhere.

. . .

I'm playing miniature golf at Thorncliffe Mall with top actor Jan-Michael Vincent, in town with his brothers Bob-Thaddeus, Troy-Cecil, Chip-Jim and Gus-Gus.

We welcome Hollywood's Chuck Connors to the Imperial Six as we show off our new 36mm film technology. The extra millimetre showcases sideburns on screen.

Zoning rules allowing for up to 16 smelting operations per ward are being grandfathered. We've got top grandfathers working on it right now.

Mrs. Xanadu now has me on an all salt-lick diet. Sez she read that Pat Nixon has her hubby on it. But the thirst!!!

Pal Robert Goulet's classy new bar, International Waters, is now open high atop Pottery Rd. The drinks flow freely, as do the recriminations!

City Council motion to introduce a 13% exorcism tax seems like a blatant cash grab to me, and will serve only to drive the exorcism industry out.

Rubes at Ontario Censor Board to ban all 'come hither' scenes. Don't they know that 35mm film going thru a projector is itself a sexual act?

Honoured to have been chosen for prestigious 'gadfly-in-residence' at Tulsa's International Sequel Hall of Fame, but must say no due to my eternal gout.

Easily-provoked but eerily-charming Richard Burton is here shooting a Woolco TV spot. He called ahead to order ice cubes just the way he likes 'em.

. . .

My Hollywood spies say Beatle Paul McCartney is set to play James Bond in 1974's *DIE AS EMERALDS DO*. Lee Marvin in as hairless villain, Gravlax.

Trying to write a filthy limerick. What rhymes with 'comptroller'?

City Council Escalator Horseplay Sub-Committee meeting postponed until 2pm.

Surveyors discover forgotten Toronto neighbourhood, Brigadoodle, under the Bloor Viaduct. Three beagles, a librarian and a foul-mouthed skate sharpener are all that's left.

Reports of a robot army approaching Toronto from the west have now been downgraded to a sighting of a busload of Buffalo dental students wearing braces.

I feel insulted when someone says the word 'rotunda' in my presence.

Intersection of King and Bay closed today for banks' annual 'Washing of the Coins'. Bring some Javex and join in the fun!

Opening tomorrow at the Imperial Six: Susan St. James, Slim Pickens and Bobby Sherman in erotic courtroom thriller *APPROACH THE BENCH*.

Last old hand at Riverdale Zoo who knew how to unthaw frozen giraffe testicles has retired, so now it's me, a footstool and cigar smoke.

It's been said that I have the strength of ten men. Each of those men is the equivalent of Don Knotts, but still, it does add up.

· · ·

Delay at TTC St. Clair due to lavender-fueled, scowl-filled status showdown, triggered by an imperceptible slight between rival dowagers.

Can't find pants that fit this morning, so I will be conducting official City business from the back seat of my limo today.

I'm reinstating the curfew on shiftless brothers-in-law. Two were spotted at Becker's in their bathrobes fighting over Lune Moons.

I'm at the Park Plaza Hotel bar with Alvin Toffler, Bobby Hull and Mel Tormé, convincing them that pencil moustaches are manly. And the trout ale is delicious!

Peter Lawford may have the biggest penis in the hemisphere, but that isn't going to get in the way of his stupendously violent fight against the Mafia's plan to take over his lucrative airline sick bag empire, in *UPRIGHT POSITION*, opening Friday at the Imperial Six.

Canadian Architectural Archives | Archives and Special Collections | University of Calgary Panda Associates fonds PAN 73245-12c. Imperial Six Theatre (Toronto) -- interior image

Patrons of my masterpiece of time-killing, the Imperial Six cinemas, love to promenade down our lower lobby staircase, a delightful ode to the one in Alfred Hitchcock's *PSYCHO* upon which Martin Balsam was murdered.

✿ 2 ✿

A TYPICAL DAY FOR A HYPNOTIC LEADER

I'm seen here parallel parking, politically speaking.

L adies and Gentlemen, boys and girls of all ages: I would like to tell you what a typical day is like for me.

I SAID: I. WOULD. LIKE. TO. TELL. YOU. WHAT. A. TYPICAL. DAY. IS. FOR. ME.!!!! GODDAMMIT!! IS THIS GODFOR-SAKEN DICTAPHONE WORKING?!?!

. . .

13

A typical day for me starts at 4:30 am when I rise, as all men do, in a state of profound unease and confusion, compounded by muscle spasms, frozen feet, and gas.

Once I am on my feet (both quickly enveloped in Simpson-Sears 'Tootsie-Wootsie' brand slipperettes), my head clears of the fog and llamas of my nightmares, and fills quickly with my responsibilities, oaths, grand schemes, and ways to milk more profit from a garbage bag full of movie theatre popcorn popped five months previous.

My Henry the Eighth-themed mohair robe upon me (it comes with *two* belts, the better to thwart errant breezes), I attend to my ablutions, a regimen of pumice, sandpaper, toupée mucilage, Pope's Choice Tooth Powder, and about thirteen towels.

But hark! Plucking that manly but distracting grey hair from the middle of my forehead must wait, as the baritone howls of my twin Irish Wolfhounds, Ossington and Islington, beckon me to address their bowel & ego needs.

To the Xanadu garden we must go – and go they do, in such prolific streams, and with such monumental deposits of night soil as to roil and oppress the neighbours.

While the dogs' terrible and odiferous business is underway, I stroll through my ornamental hedge maze, an exact 1/1000 scale replica of the streets of downtown Toronto as they were on the day of my birth, January 1, 1911 (with long-gone landmarks like the Shriners' Stockades and the Open-Toed Shoe Polish Museum depicted with armour discarded by the Royal Ontario Museum, and papier-mâché). My thoughts at this time are many and varied, a jumble of vendettas and re-zonings I've planned for the day ahead.

I've assembled by now all these many wisps of purpose and meaning into a crystalline art deco diamond orb of action and strategy in my head (I'd love it as a set of cufflinks, actually!!). My heart, gut, brain, tongue and fists are now poised to collaboration on what could be the single-greatest day of my 27 Toronto mayoralty terms of office.

My gentle beasts' excretions concluded, I now dash to my walk-in suit humidor to don my armour for the day's battles ahead. Arrayed before me are 300 + suits, enough to clad a small but potent mercenary army of well-dressed mercenaries.

The three-piece Louis Prima-brand cross-hatched Cuff Master? Too showy. The waterproof two-piece belted steam-room Conversational-ist? Too casual. The tin-crease, tarp-cloth Black Hole-black Negotiator (with hidden hip-flask caddy and Bakelite waistcoat?) Just right.

And so, with the addition of a rage-patterned necktie and Anaconda-wingtip shoes, I race to my Telex machine, for my city sleeps even less than I do. Inevitably, a pile of pleas, subpoenas, police blotter high-lights and Chow Mein menus are neatly-stacked beside the grey elec-tronic communications behemoth, having been sorted in order of winsomeness by my night secretary Mrs. Dorothy Lauderdale (she has not slept since the War).

Do I approve a request to place decorative Hawaiian leis on all city hydrants to honour visiting Hollywood thespian Jack Lord? Of course! Should I visit the scene of a dastardly 1:00 a.m. heist at the Bick's Pickle Factory? You couldn't keep me away! Shall I extend the violent-taining Thai razor blade action pic *PULVERIZE* for a 27th week at the Imperial Six? Its star, pal Peter Lawford, would expect nothing less!

Decisions! They flow from me like clouds of hairspray from Joey Heatherton. But now to action. Gathering my mayorly-manly-show-manly accoutrements – spare cufflinks, five fountain pens, two crisp hankies and mother-in-law-of-pearl cigarette holder, — I perambulate to my waiting limousine, revved ever so gently by my driver of 32 years, Tartat, a former French legionnaire and children's entertainer.

· · ·

The back seat of the specially-equipped 1963 Chevrolet Biscayne is a plush parallel universe, containing miniaturized or simply cheaper versions of mostly everything that's in my City Hall office (modelled after Charles de Gaulle's), and my Imperial Six office (modelled after Charles Foster Kane's).

My comely but terrifying secretary Barbara Von Barbara (surprisingly sophisticated for a native of Leaside) is already on the jump seat, ready to take dictation or draw a courtroom-artist-type depiction of my flights of fancy (e.g. a fleet of City zeppelins to provide shade to redheads and their sensitive skin).

And we're off! My secret route takes us up Merton St. to Mt. Pleasant Rd., south past my alma mater, the former Mt. Pleasant Cemetery High School (now an obsequity training school for undertakers), rolling down into the dirt paths of David Balfour Park (I'm in a hurry!) up and then across the Rosehill Reservoir, to Yonge St., then barreling down to Queen St., stopping only for some unscheduled kibitzing with the common man along the way and shazam! - we drive up the ramp at City Hall and down the private elevator to my office. It's 11:15 a.m. and I am fired up and ready to go, no crowing cocks to disturb me!

But first, a pre-lunch cocktail with my allies on City Council. This is a daily ritual that goes back, some say, to first parliament in faraway Iceland, where alcohol was needed to pronounce all the consonants in their legislative debates.

Able men all, they gather before me, drinks and neckties in hand, as I bark out their marching orders for the afternoon's council session. Vote NO! on the Puppet Theatre Demolition By-Law! Vote YES! on the gerrymandering of the Sea Shanty District on Ward's Island! Vote NO! on the $8 million dollar steam-cleaning contract for the CNE Pure Food Building. And so forth.

Their confidence bolstered, their duties clear, we can all now retire to the mountainous platters of rare roast beef, deported horseradish, and canoe-sized eclairs on offer at Old Ed's. Before you and your lower intestines know it, it's 3 p.m., and the people's work must be done!

Another session of City Council is called to order, in the airy if somewhat psychotropic chambers. What unfolds is, while legal and all that, a cross between a physiotherapy hospital's amateur performance of Gilbert and Sullivan's *UTOPIA, LIMITED* and a Richard Burton/Liz Taylor gin-provoked donnybrook. The screaming alone could drive you mad, or home.

But, through my mastery of hand signals, raised eyebrows, staged tantrums, walk-outs, chair-kicking and the unexpurgated edition of Robert's Rules of Order, our legislative agenda is rammed through as speedily as the Centreville log flume ride during a sun shower.

The 50-minute session concluded, the bodies counted, and the bile mopped up, I return to my office for private meetings about public matters, during which Toronto's and the world's top men and dazzling womenfolk seek my counsel, my blessing, and my largesse (said to be the province's largest).

Consider, if you will, this sample agenda picked at random from a recent day's labour by a blindfolded Barbara von Barbara, just to prove its randomness:

-4pm: meet Mr. Dirk Bottomsby, General Mgr. of Gothic Brothers Halloween Mask Company of Eglinton Ave. East. Wishes to ask Mayor Xanadu if there are circumstances under which it is legal to murder a City building inspector.

-4:03 p.m.: meet representative of the Sisterhood of Municipal Cafeteria Workers, who wish to complain, in bitter terms, of the newly added strain imposed upon them by the Mayor's demand to have all menu items available in fried versions.

. . .

-4:45 p.m.: present the Key to the City to visiting British actor Terry-Thomas, appearing at the Colonnade Theatre in the bathroom farce *THE MISSUS DROPPED HER WASHCLOTH, WOT?*

As the clock at Old City Hall chimes 5pm (I've had it set five minutes fast, to thin out rush hour), my civic duties are done -- but my showman responsibilities are about to begin! Many have asked, or been encouraged to ask, just how I make the mental and physical transition from the weighty and sober challenges of being a mayor to the no-less weighty but hypnotically entertaining role of chief showman at the Imperial Six cinemas.

Think of a Belgian bank teller who moonlights as a waffle house drag queen. Think of a sturdy oak tree being harvested and transmuted into an emperor's throne. Think of the steaming unpasteurized milk streaming out of contented Andorran cow being pixilated into a towering cream cheese cheesecake. That's all me.

But, from 5 to 6pm daily, as I strip off my civic cares and bicameral bifocals in favour of a Cary Grant 'Count Rushmore' tuxedo, and James Wong Howe-approved indoor sunglasses, I remind myself that my two jobs, my two personas, are not so different, I and me.

I rule the City of Toronto like a Broadway impresario – competitive, flashy, and treating every dull municipal day as if it's opening night.

I run the Imperial Six like a mayor, aware that my patrons are my voters, free to switch allegiances to any Thalberg-come-lately who might very well *promise* that the films will start on time, but is, in reality, incapable of herding slothful projectionists, pimpleton ushers, sugar-coated candy girls and sleight-of-handy box office cashiers into anything approaching a 'schedule'.

I am like Dr. Jekyll and Mr. Hyde, but without need of a flask of vile chemicals nor painful gyrations to transform myself. I just am.

$\cdot\ \cdot\ \cdot$

Those plaintive cries you hear at 5pm are not those of moody beasts complaining about the quality of the Riverdale Zoo gruel. No – these are the cries of the people, people whose daily labours, be they chiropodists of chiaroscurists, be they plate-spinners or spinsters, be they worm pickers or spineless husbands, put them in such a state of lassitude as to force them to cry out for entertainment! That's where I come in.

Chauffeured in a vintage Sam Snead golf cart either by a police officer (City Hall to Imperial Six) or by an usher (Imperial Six to City Hall), I traverse the 1000 yards between my municipal day and my cinematic night, and sometimes back again, through my private tunnel, its walls decorated with alternating framed photos of former mayors and of Rin Tin Tin).

By the time I arrive in the ancient subterranean Twizzler caves 'neath the Imperial Six (archeologists say, as if anyone is listening, that this was once the site of pre-historic hand gesture festivals) my tuxedo is the badge of my arsenal of showmanship. It serves as my armour of gregariousness, my condom of conviviality, if you will. But also as an assurance, a walking, talking, smoking, joking logo of guaranteed entertainment ("Peter Lawford's latest, *GUT PUNCH*, anyone?") – to the Imperial Six's patrons that their evening will be well spent, their greasy cares and picayune problems washed away in a glaze of pasteurized cinematic splendour.

It's showtime, Dolores!!

City of Toronto Archives, Fonds 1034, Item 2

I remember when all the mailmen in Toronto named Percival would gather once a month across the street from the city's sole burlesque theatre, the Tassel Castle on Davisville Ave., and try to work up the nerve to go in. But they never did.

GENERAL HOORAY, CANADA'S ONLY CELEBRITY MAGAZINE

Supping at the city's only salamander chili cafe on chic Overlea Blvd. Decor is ancient Mayan -- as are the prices!

Soup of the Day in Toronto tomorrow: Boil of Olay.

I'm wearing my orthopaedic toupée today. It helps lift my mind out of the gutter.

When shovelling snow, lift with your hips and crotch, and decisively pivot, swivel, hoist, thrust and release, as one does during sex.

Colonel Sanders in town today to 'interview' some chickens.

. . .

Tonite on *MANNIX*: Joe spends the entire episode in a lineup to renew his driver's licence, thinking, "there's got to be a better way."

Due to icy conditions, the Gardiner Expressway exit ramps are especially exit-y this morning.

Toronto is the Fred MacMurray of cities -- sometimes the *MY THREE SONS* Fred, but sometimes, just sometimes, the sexy *DOUBLE INDEMNITY* Fred.

In honour of Groundhog Day, all elevators in the city will rise slowly, hesitate on the ground floor, then return to the basement.

If the Mob thinks they can move in on Peter Lawford's Guam courier business, they've got another thing coming... and another... and another... in *SIGN HERE, HERE AND HERE TO DIE*, opening Friday at the Imperial Six.

Local restaurantrepreneur Tony Ontario's city-wide chain of eating establishments --- from the Mackintosh Toffee cafeteria on Pape Ave. to the crustless bread nightclub on Dufferin --- are so popular that he is now operating his own menu tassel factory!

I'm just landing at Malton Airport. Flight from Los Angeles marred by in-flight screening of Bruce Dern/Mae West flop *GORILLA DROPPINGS*.

Fun Fact: Toronto's R.C. Harris Water and Urine Filtration Plant can be viewed from outer space, although it rarely is.

. . .

Shipped two more scrofulous Imperial Six projectionists off to the drunk tank -- caught 'em sniffing silver nitrate and splicing Lee Marvin into kids' cartoons.

When I need to 'lower' my masculinity, I rely on Bobcaygeon's Own Testosterone Leeches, the old-timey way to keep rage and desire locked up!

Opening this week at the Imperial Six: Cliff Robertson, Cliff Gorman, Cliff Richard and Jimmy Cliff in cliff-hanger *THE CLIFFS OF NAVARONE.*

TTC emergency code 455 = a musty and metallic absinthe smell on streetcar. Also referred to as a 'Barnaby Jones'.

Due to the extreme cold weather this week, the City's emergency supply of theatrical merkins and fright wigs are now available to those with goosebumps.

Polishing the wrecking ball as we prepare to demolish the 37-storey art deco Mary Pickford Doll Hospital to make way for a Humidor College.

Toronto's oldest and final vaudeville comedy duo, Parsnip and Piccadilly, are desperately touring old-age homes collecting mother-in-law material.

My twin Irish wolfhounds, Ossington and Islington, are majestic in their countenance, but amoeba-like in their understanding.

I'm in Timmins for annual meeting of the Stanchion and Velvet Rope Manufacturers Association. It's so cold here my bank account is frozen! (I kid).

· · ·

In the next issue of General Hooray (Canada's sole domestic celebrity magazine) we ask Paul Anka "When did you stop caring?"

TTC passengers: let the people off the trains first. Then you can scratch and claw yerselves to death getting on, I don't care.

Remember the 1940s actioners I directed and starred in, the *CHICK CHESTERFIELD: TORONTO DICK* serials? Just found the 35mm prints in the basement of the Donlands People's Kinotorium! They were perfectly preserved in Twizzler residue!

I've proven the naysayers wrong again! Now that TTC King streetcars have battering rams, cowcatchers, air horns, spitball cannons and Grauman's Chinese Theatre klieg lights, 1.7 minutes has been shaved off the Melinda St. to Toronto St. commute!

My hand-picked blue-ribbon panel has completed its two-year investigation 'Cause of the Ted Reeve Arena Stink'. Their conclusion? It's Larry. It's always been Larry.

City barge carrying 600 tons of winter squirrel feces from Centre Island has hit a goose and is marooned. This could delay spring.

I shot the ninth *CHICK CHESTERFIELD: TORONTO DICK* pic in Elbow-rama, which used on-screen prompts to urge moviegoers to jab their sleeping pals.

I'm at Malton Airport welcoming a delegation of Yield Sign Traffic Engineers from Bulgaria, here to study our world-class level of obedience.

· · ·

On my feet at the Scientific Gents' Hospital after my annual donation of excess testosterone. I'm pant-less, downing a handsome sirloin steak and a pint of V.I.P. prune juice.

This afternoon I'll be at the Island Airport to greet the first flight of Air Confederation's thrice-monthly one-way service from Toledo (planes are towed back there by truck).

This Friday at the Imperial Six: Paul Anka and Liza Minnelli star in traveller's' cheques heist pic *THE UMLAUT COHORT*. However, we can't reproduce an actual umlaut on the marquee.

Speaking to the Oshawa Gravel, Asphalt and Detritus Guild on topic: 'Rubble: The Bastard Son Your Industry Needs to Acknowledge'.

Hot ticket at the Imperial Six! Shelley Winters, Shelley Berman and Shelley Fabares in Sheldon Leonard's *BOLT UPRIGHT*, an inadvertently erotic take on Mary Shelley's Frankenstein.

City-wide alert: a mud hen has escaped from Riverdale Farm. He has a taste for blood, and answers to the name 'Dennis'.

My elite Imperial Six ushers are elated if exhausted after an overnight 'war game' exercise I put them through: changing every cinema marquee to italics and back.

Shocking in its lascivious disregard for human decency, the would-be High Park Nudist Colony has applied for a grant to map poison ivy bushes.

I'm cutting the ribbon to open a salamander abattoir on Mutual St., largest in the British Commonwealth. What's that stink? The stink of success!

· · ·

Rife with non-gratuitous violence, lawn bowling is now brought to the big screen with tenderness and Teamsters in Sam Peckinpah's epic *GRASS STAIN REVULSION*, with Dan Blocker and Lorna Luft, opening Friday at the Imperial Six.

Action has a name, and its name is Geoff Bunsen, formerly Geoffrey Bunsen, but shortened in error by his divorce lawyer. Star Peter Lawford metes out justice in tiny but bloody quantities in *GEOFF: THE G IS SILENT*, Friday at the Imperial Six.

In Victorian Toronto, a gentleman would seek to woo a lady by sending her a daguerreotype of his raised eyebrows through a de-eroticizing public notary intermediary.

In one of my 1937 *CHICK CHESTERFIELD: TORONTO DICK* episodes, *LEASIDE LOOSENS ITS TROUSERS*, I punch that troubled municipality's ersatz chicken salad mogul, Legs Akimbo, right in the imlach.

City expected to coagulate by 4pm.

I've instructed City of Toronto employees to increase their use of the word 'moot'.

A sad day as Toronto's final Prime Minister William Lyon Mackenzie King look-alike shop, Grey Jowl, is going out of business, a victim of fickle youth, and the Louis St. Laurent cult.

Tonite on *TOUPÉE COP*: Bruno uncovers a scam exploiting men whose hair on the back of their necks won't go up, even when chilled by suspense: the bogus neckpée.

· · ·

Chimps at Riverdale Zoo no longer 'fling' their feces at visitors, but it's now obvious that putting tiny catapults in their cages was a mistake.

Tonite on *IRONSIDE*: Raymond Burr shoots a promo, but insists on wearing a balaclava, "to add suspense."

To hurry democracy along, the following Toronto wards will be consolidated, transmogrified or eliminated: St. Durward-Pure Food Building; Merton Coal Silo; Varsity Stadium-Mr. Submarine; Photostat District; The Cliffs of Pape. Govern yourselves accordingly.

Due to the extremely cold temperatures today, all Shetland ponies in the City of Toronto must be kept indoors and consoled.

I've ordered City skating rinks to play only Frank Sinatra Jr. songs, nothing by Sinatra himself. The elder's singing is too insistent and could lead to showboating.

Delay at TTC St. Clair station due to 1000-page unread copy of the Leon Uris novel, *THE CHRYSANTHEMUM PERTURBATION*, falling on the tracks, has now cleared.

Henry Moore's sculpture 'The Archer' at City Hall is dynamic and profound. He'll be pissed off when he learns I've put a skate-sharpening booth in front of it.

Ticketed and towed from city streets this morning: Mrs. Pat Wherewithal's 1959 Mercury Turnpike Fingerling (needs a wash), Mr. Ed Chloro's 1971 Dodge Buddy Ebsenmobile (copyright violation), and a truck owned by Gut Wrench Tablets (whiff of danger).

Opening a new library branch in the converted CNE 'Laff In The Dark' ride, housing collection of books on terror, petulance and sugar.

. . .

Attention projectionists: Provincial Police are here to collect your urine, stool and drool samples. Honest men have nothing to fear!

Opening at the Imperial Six: ham radio heist pic *THE ALPHA BRAVO CHARLIE DELTA ECHO FOXTROT GOLF HOTEL INDIA JULIET KILO LIMA MIKE CAPER.*

I've found that when a motion picture has a head title card reading 'A film by', popcorn sales plummet by 63%.

Although Hollywood rewards such behaviour, in my city we levy a $35 fine for unctuous pandering.

Swiss Consul-General and I are cutting the ribbon at the opening of the new Swiss Chalet Restaurant. She tells me their chickens are flown here first class from Davos.

My Hollywood spies tell me macho Sean Connery so enjoyed his *ZARDOZ* loincloth he now wears nothing else! (You heard me right, ladies!!).

Doctor's got me on an all butter and licorice diet. He'd better not be using me as a guinea pig bet with his golf club buddies!

My twin wolfhounds Ossington and Islington are howling in joy at the mailman this morning - the new issue of *Dog's Business* magazine has arrived!

Racoon infiltration of City Hall - they now control key sectors of the third floor and loading dock - is intolerable. Memos will be issued.

. . .

Elvis is back! And this time he's buck naked in the Swedish hospital romp *FLÄSKPROBE (PAGING DR. BACON)*, now playing at the Imperial Six.

Another marriage proposal arrives from Doris Day. I reject her for the same reason as always: she's always winking in the goddamn enclosed foto.

I've been asked to serve as peacemaker between the warring Humidifiers Association and Dehumidifiers Guild. The bloodshed must stop!!

For years I've eaten precisely one dozen processed cheese slices every day at 5:30 pm. This reminds me of the quiet nobility of cows, and I move on.

City mouse catcher union boss at my door, usual complaints: don't do rats, allergic to cheese, whiskers are creepy, worm pickers earn more etc., etc., etc., zzzzzzzzzz…

Ethel Turp, City Hall's oldest cafeteria cook, turns 99 today, still 'beets' the rest! Knew Earl of Sandwich personally, sez he was a slob.

To relieve overcrowding on the TTC Yonge line, passengers are asked to sell their homes and move to less crowded areas of the city.

Robert Goulet, Paul Anka, Lloyd Bochner, Bruno Gerussi, Lorne Greene, Murray Westgate and Burton Cummings are The Group of Several, arty painters struggling against dunce-like critics, ouchy sleet, and the impatience of the gods in *WATCHING PAINT DRY WHILE I CRY*, now at the Imperial Six.

·   ·   ·

Fun Fact: in Victorian Toronto the Don River was used to float doubtful ideas.

Slight delay on TTC Yonge line as it switches over to the Gregorian calendar.

Companies are reminded that tomorrow is Spruce Up Your Loading Dock Day in Toronto. A Tiffany lamp, a heartbreakingly lovely paisley rug, a shpritz of Pomilot sauce - - anything to ameliorate the incessant and pointless loading and unloading for the working man.

Tomorrow's Soup of the Day in Toronto: Horny Chowder.

City of Toronto Archives, Fonds 1257, Series 1057, Item 3849

Glamorous mourning veil model Ethel Fabulist inaugurates Toronto's swanky Quick Dry Cement Museum, a testament to man's impatience. That's me standing behind egomaniacal cement magnate C. C. Heliocentric, who evades property taxes by never letting the cement actually dry.

IT'S 'CYRILLIC TYPEWRITER
DAY' IN TORONTO

On my second Franburger as Pierre Berton drones on about some pick-axe or donkey that changed Confederation. He's lost the 'bore war' with me!

Mrs. Xanadu forced me to try on the 'trendy' new Dom DeLuise-brand 'Freelax' aqua leisure suits. Made me look like a jumbo jet in a diaper!

. . .

The City's first lake-going raft of spring sent to Ward's Island finds marooned residents hairy, ornery, unable to 'get' current limericks, and addicted to Tahiti Treat.

Dropping by the Pape St. Recalcitrant Male Readers' Library. Just *MAD* Magazines, cereal boxes and Burt Reynolds biographies so far, but it's a start!

Tonite on *TOUPÉE COP*: Bruno enjoys a moment of job satisfaction as the 80-foot-high bonfire of counterfeit toupées burns lustily into the night.

I'm busy, as usual this time of year, helping Hollywood stars with their Oscars concession speeches.

Sleet is the sexiest of the precipitations.

Don't forget to turn your clocks back tonight to a time when everything made sense.

Opening today at the Imperial Six: Czech monastery heist pic *PATHOLOGICAL FRIAR*.

In Victorian Toronto, March came in like a Jules Verne mechanical succubus, and went out like a gravy-stained ottoman.

Delay at TTC Bloor is society's fault.

There is no place where one can see a panoramic view of Toronto, although the city can be sufficiently apprehended from any spot.

· · ·

I am insisting that there will be legal limits placed on those foodstuffs which may be caramelized, and those which may not.

Top men of science tell me that moping is here to stay.

When passion rears its hideously seductive head can cardboard keep Dan Blocker and Charo apart? *CORRUGATED LOVERS*, now at the Imperial Six.

Embargo the Clown's back and Sayvette's got 'im! — at 89 years young! Enjoy his balloon animals (only ostrich egg and snakes at this time) and wacky shrieks of arthritic pain.

Soup of the Day in Toronto is Paroled Beets.

The City's coddled road salt workers refuse my efficiency tips (e.g. moving their asses faster), due to the power of their global salt union, which includes farm salt lick workers, tear ductologists, salt & vinegar chip stevedores, and salty language strip club comedians.

My Imperial Six ushers are now wearing Soviet industrial mittens made for ushers changing marquee letters at the Yakutsk Bijou at minus 73°. Butane, whale blubber and mink are involved!

I'm at Malton Airport waiting to board my Air Apparent flight to Los Angeles for the Oscars. I'll be Carol Burnett's earlobe prompter.

My Oscars cummerbunds are made from Mortal Sin Black Luxe Saran Wrap, to allow for maximum indulgence and circumference.

I'll be at Hollywood's swankiest hotel, The Dowager's Inherited Tiara, next to Soupy Sales' Tie Blotch shtick restaurant.

Tragedy averted at pre-Oscars brunch as John Wayne almost choked to death on a crouton. Doctors say he is cursing comfortably.

Surprised to learn that Yul Brynner brings his own seat-filler to the Oscars, a wax dummy of himself crossing his legs in agony.

Mike 'Mannix' Connors shows real class by agreeing to mime laryngitic Strother Martin's Oscars acceptance speech.

Fun Oscars Fact: there are five working tinsel mines on the outskirts of Whittier, California that solely serve Hollywood.

Don Adams and I are sharing a limo to the Mrs. Dorothy Lauderdale Pavilion. He tells me his new sitcom *NOSE HAIR* has been pre-cancelled.

En route to the Oscars we stop to pick up Carol Channing and Bud Cort, whose *BEN HUR*-themed rickshaw (pulled by Bud) has shed its papier-mâché cladding.

Fun Fact: the Oscars red carpet is hand-woven from the pink slips given to hundreds of Marlon Brando's former valets. The man is a pig.

Raquel Welch's perfume, 'Liquid Cleavage', is causing men to drop to their knees here on the Oscars red carpet.

Foreigner Oscars nominees Ingmar Bergman and Bernardo Bertolucci are speaking together on the red carpet in some weirdo patois to exclude us all.

· · ·

At the bar with Paul McCartney and 5/8 of his rock music band Wings. They'll perform an Oscars tribute to stage fright alongside the banjo kid from *DELIVERANCE*.

Red Buttons never fails to crack me up with his wacky antics -- but I think his blood-curdling fall from the Oscars balcony just now was unintentional.

Henry Fonda, Jane Fonda, Peter Fonda, Chip Fonda, Adolph Fonda and Wanda Fonda are having a loud family argument in the lobby here at the Oscars. Ugh.

Oscars host Lee Majors' wooden personality shines thru in the opening musical number "Hollywood's Ladies of the Blacklist".

Best Supporting Actress winner Joey Heatherton shocks with an acceptance speech in computer language Cobol.

Cinematographer Sven Nykvist gets a laugh when he admits he added the two 'v's to his names to impress girls.

I am amused to learn that smarmy pretty-boy Robert Redford has six layers of pancake makeup on. Bet that *THE STING*'s a bit!

Producer shot by Clint Eastwood in the lobby earlier almost made it into the Oscars 'In Memoriam' tribute.

Klaus Kinski and Helen Reddy presenting the Academy Award for Best Splice. They have no chemistry.

Eddie Albert just decked Telly Savalas for using 'Gabor' as an obscene verb.

Canada's own — and only domestic film director — Norman Jewison reveals to me that Tony Curtis uses a prosthetic personality.

While urinating adjacent to me, Francis Ford Coppola sez he's signed to direct the *BARNABY JONES* movie.

Lorne Greene, nominated tonight as the ambisexual mime in *CABARET*, tells me his upcoming *EARTHQUAKE* pic will make rubble sexy.

Shelley Winters' blatant lobbying for Oscars votes backfires after she walks into the auditorium on her hands to recreate a scene from *THE POSEIDON ADVENTURE*.

Not that I am a prude, but seeing Liza Minnelli and Benny Hill playing tongue hockey here in the Oscars lobby is in no way cinematic.

Under-the-breath booing as Lee Marvin spoils his *DIRTY DOZEN 2: DRY SHAVE THIS* Oscars acceptance speech with a filthy limerick about Spiro Agnew.

Andy Williams and Perry Como duet 'When Hollywood Hums' is not being broadcast and they don't know it.

Sad to see 87% of the cast of *LAUGH-IN* working at the coat check here at the Oscars.

Frank Sinatra is here with three people in the Witness Protection Program, so they are wearing Willy Wonka masks.

· · ·

Awkward moment on the red carpet as the Smothers Brothers bump into the Nixon Brothers (Dick and Donald).

Burt Lancaster tells me he's had a nonstop erection since 1957 and it's no picnic.

Looking forward to Ed McMahon's a cappella rendition of the Oscar-winning *THEME FROM SHAFT* tonite.

Dapper but autocratic David Niven tells me he carries a plastic shrunken head in his pocket to remind him never to badmouth Hollywood.

Elke Sommer and Jack Valenti presenting Best Foreign Language Oscar -- she'll handle the vowels, he'll take care of the consonants.

Bea Arthur and Peter Boyle presenting here at the Oscars, but dressed in gold leotards as Comedy and Tragedy, so it's a tragedy.

The Academy has invited losing nominees to read their acceptance speeches to the busboys at 2 a.m.

Burt Reynolds is up for Best Use of a Penis.

What will the Oscars decide is the Best Picture of 1973? I voted for Lorne Greene's directing debut *TUNDRAGASM*.

I'm noshing at post-Oscars bash at the George Gobel Executrix Motel. Bill Bixby is looking green, and I don't mean in a *HULK* way.

·   ·   ·

Ernest Borgnine just walked through the lobby of Statler-Crouton Hotel in a thong. This Oscars is done.

Fun Fact: Lieutenant Governor John Graves Simcoe's flatulent ghost haunts TTC Bathurst station, but with no contemporary references he thinks he's at a brothel in Leeds in 1793.

I'm visiting humourless Rosedale to chide the millionaires. Air is thinner up here. Also thin here: skin, comb-overs, wives, and excuses.

I am startled by the increase in numbers of public places in Toronto that smell like hamster cage shavings -- up 37% over 1972!?

Tomorrow I'll be cutting the ribbon at the official opening of Human Carbolic's massive new factory on Spadina, where their popular prison shampoo, Quell, is made!

TTC Pape bus has gone rogue, spotted on 401 at 85 MPH. Driver is shouting out the window to police that he has a shy bladder, so can only pee at home.

St. Patrick's Day Parade clean-up in Toronto hampered by potato debris and leprechaun dandruff.

Sharing a jeroboam of Belgian drinker's wine with Mike Connors, TV's *MANNIX*, here shooting a safety video for Brewer's Retail accountants.

Usher alert! Usher alert! There is a man in Theatre 5 'buttering his popcorn'. Eject him with extreme prejudice.

· · ·

Opening today: Lee Van Cleef, Harvey Lembeck, Marjoe Gortner and Dame Edith Evans in minimum security prison break thriller *THE CELL DOOR IS AJAR.*

City Hall's new Paper Tiger Industrial Stapler, a retrofitted Zamboni, can easily staple a 3000-page document, e.g. The Upanishads, or volumes of shoeshine by-laws.

My twin Irish Wolfhounds, Ossington and Islington, generate enough manure to fertilize a farm in County Kerry. It's getting it there that's the problem.

I am pleased to officially declare tomorrow Cyrillic Typewriter Day which ---- goddammit, who the hell am I kidding? No one gives a rat's ass!!!

I heartily endorse Balder-Dash©, the scalp tonic for men who are bald, and want to stay that way!

In Victorian Toronto, people knew spring was nigh when their backyard chickens started pecking each other's genitals as if to say "love me."

Fun Fact: the tar used to pave Toronto's streets is made from hippie guitars seized at unlicensed go-go taverns.

My new punishment for mouthy ushers: strap 'em to a seat for viewing of nine hours of old Buddy Ebsen pics. I call it 'A Clockwork Prune'.

Reading the Kinsey Report (wowsa!) to pass the time at Dave Keon's Pants-Pressed-While-U-Wait. Is there a breeze in here or is it just me?

• • •

I was a back-of-the head stand-in for top Hollywood stars in the 1930's. My pleasing head-shape and nodding skills earned me top dollar!

At stupefyingly boring Council debate re: auxiliary police uniform epaulettes. My mind drifts to thoughts of Paula Prentiss....

Found so far in melted snowbanks: 67 copies of *THE VALACHI PAPERS*; 523 pieces of Sonny and Cher Halloween candy; a guy named Mel.

My annual Public Verbal Abuse of Ushers has been nixed by a Trudeau government human rights-type. I like the man's style, but fer chrissakes Pierre, grow a pair!

Before 6pm, I call them 'trousers'. After 6pm I call them 'slacks'.

Soup of the Day in Toronto is Potable Drizzle.

Doctor sez my 43 daily cups of joe are what's keeping me up at night. I'll tell you what's keeping me up: werewolves, jazz and ingratitude.

I'm part Irish, part Transylvanian, meaning that I have a big heart, but you'd have to drive a wooden stake through it to shut me up.

City of Toronto Archives, Fonds 124, File 1, Item 122

Our glistening city, so regal and rambunctious, yet contained within stone, while coyly teasing us with the stone of the future: plastic.

5

INFRASTRUCTURE? DON'T MIND IF I DO!

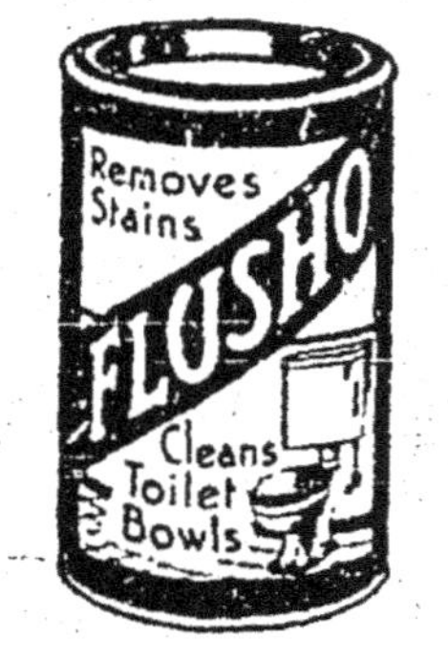

T here is a secret city. Behind the Toronto you endure each day lies another city, one known only to the megalapolitan cognoscenti. But I'm not going to write about that today.

Instead, I will celebrate the sinewy and sewagy infrastructure of the City of Toronto and its skeletal underpinnings ---pipes, wires, troughs, spittoons, and curbettes --- that keep this town functioning and from collapsing into itself, like a misbegotten sponge cake. It is estimated— for no one truly knows --- that 79 per cent of your tax dollars go to maintaining and ruthlessly expanding this infrastructure. As you faint backwards upon reading this, be assured that it is the infrastructure itself that will break your fall, and perhaps your coccyx.

Like your random thoughts about orangutans and trousers, the municipal layers of steel, stone, and stucco are intricately interwoven, yet show an uncallous disregard for one another and an aloofness that ensures efficiency.

Deepest down, far below our saliva-drenched sidewalks, are the Lord Simcoe Caves of Refuse—huge and spooky rock-holes where garbage too unmentionable even to burn is tossed and forgotten, usually via the Pape Avenue Hole to the Centre of the Earth. The Caves are manned by just one employee, who is supplied with manly blankets and a stack of remaindered pre-Confederation novels. Above this hideous stratum lie the Regional Purgatorial Flames, a natural if satanic source of geothermal heat for some of the city's reform schools (whose pesky residents can't complain of the sulphurous aroma, due to strict no-talking-back rules).

Then we rise to the enchanting Utter Under River, an underground stream discovered by drunken plumbers in 1921. An especially sweet and pure stream of crystal clear water, it is diverted solely to the bidets of local titans of industry, because. Above that rest the rust-enhanced pipes that deliver the city's drinking and bathing water, direct from a small frog-popular creek near Pottery Road and not from Lake Ontario, as is widely believed.

We now surface, our eyes blinking in the piercing but temporary sunshine. While citizens might be familiar with the roads that criss-cross our great metropolis, they probably don't know that most were forged by rival criminal gangs in the early 20th century, each vying to craft the most efficacious escape routes to vamoose, along with their filthy spoils. If not for their evil ways, we'd not have a way to drive to Barrie.

· · ·

Visible every 10 miles or so along the boulevards are gold-plated hydrants, each handcrafted in the Fabergé eggeries of St. Petersburg but painted a dull yellow colour to fool speculators. But our eyes are now drawn up, as if by boredom or a hunt for a decent pie shop, to the towering poles of power, or 'power poles', which transmit hydro-electricity to each and every bill-paying home and business, to do with we know not what.

These crucial layers, along with other infrastructural delights such as ventriloquism schools, white-collar crime dry cleaners, police dog romperies, and road salt camp cinemas, are among the many elements of a modern city that you just don't need to think about. We do the thinking for you.

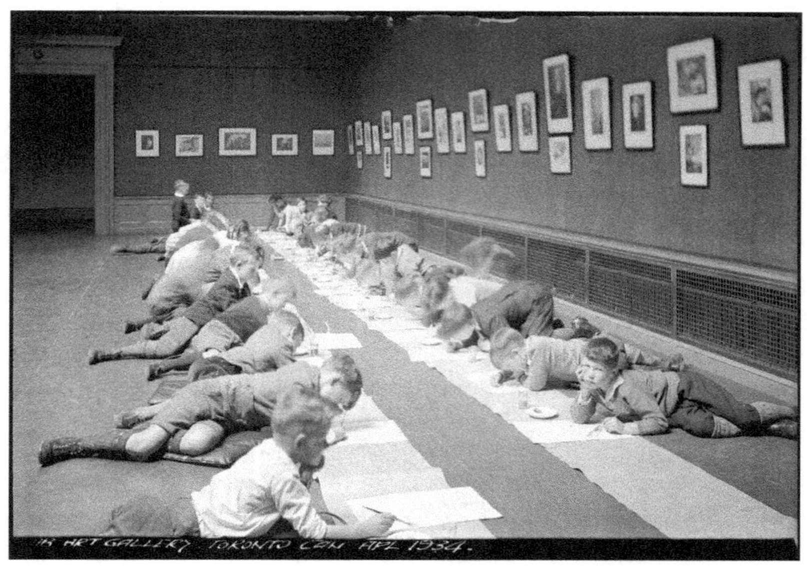

City of Toronto Archives, Fonds 200, Series 372, Subseries 2, Item 18

When I was a lad, we saved up our pennies to enrol in sick note forgery classes at the Pape Ave. House of Anarchy.

6

OSCAR-BAIT PAUL ANKA IN 'THE ESOPHAGUS CALCULATION'

Tabling this idea at City Council: install European-movie-style police sirens in all our squad cars for panache. Use only on rainy nights?

TTC subway tunnel-boring machine working on the Chester station extension has gone rogue, last seen heading towards Guelph.

PULVERIZE, the extraordinarily violent razor blade heist pic, extended for another bloodmazing week! Manly star Peter Lawford is here signing bandages!

. . .

TTC emergency bus now on Yonge St. is picking up chilly men who thought spring had arrived and so went outside today wearing flimsy windbreakers.

Sleet knows it will soon be slush, so it's just lashing out at society.

Police raid Peter St. warehouse and seize 37,000 counterfeit moist towelettes. Each contained only a bay leaf and some spit.

Tonite on *TOUPÉE COP*: Bruno tracks down a ferret hair smuggling gang, and reaches a horrifying yet very comb-able conclusion.

TTC Pape station delay due to some snooty looks from a highfalutin dame setting off a rube with a chip on his shoulder has now cleared.

Good news: Toronto Island ferry service is now on its spring schedule. Bad news: the ferries are broken, so you'll be riding on the Simcoe St. Goatworks Offal and Gristle Scow.

I have decreed that Toronto will henceforth have control of the naming of constellations over our city, e.g. the Big Dipper is now Reginald.

Tonite on *IRONSIDE*: Raymond Burr's wheelchair is turned away from the camera for the whole time, due to a contract dispute.

Five valiant Imperial Six ushers were injured last night in a battle with the violent gang, The Lady Simcoes. Blood donors welcome at our Victoria St. entrance.

Traffic diverted as Mt. Pleasant has been flooded with excuses.

· · ·

Fanticipating tonite's show at the Royal York Imperial Room: Vincent Price sings German sea shanties in his ein-man show 'In The Key of Huh?'

How long would it take for an ice sculpture of Goldie Hawn to melt in a sauna? I'm just asking.

Noshing with the lovely Margaret Atwood at Kresge's. Sez her next novel will be written in the fifth person. OK by me as long as it's a cracking good potboiler!

How many roads must a man walk down before they call him a man? We're tackling that today in the Roads and Masculinity Sub-committee at City Council.

Dined at Old Ed's tonite with Cher, minus Sonny. Had the Ham Steak with peas served 'del monte' style from the tin, as is the fashion.

Opening tomorrow at the Imperial Six: Frank Gorshin, Micky Dolenz and Topo Gigio in WWII tank battle epic *FODDER KNOWS BEST.*

Traffic lights out at Pape and Queen. Drivers are to proceed with hesitancy and caution, as though they were debutantes at a Prussian cotillion ball.

Delay on TTC College streetcar due to awkward silence.

City's surplus sale: 50-lb. slabs of observation deck telescope lubricant; aldermen's handkerchief laundromat neon signage; a selection of geese.

Reports of wet socks, broken promises coming in from Ossington Ave.

. . .

He may be trapped in a runaway hot air balloon but Eddie Albert has a tuba lesson to finish in *BLOW ME DOWN*, at the Imperial Six on Friday.

I gave up sneezing, chewing and standing for Lent, but I'm paying the price now.

A broken escalator isn't going to stop Michael Landon in his quest for a cure for horniness in *REACH FOR THE PANTS*, at the Imperial Six.

Toronto has the highest number of unlowered Murphy beds in the world.

I will be guest host this week of CFTO-TV's final black and white game show *PLACATE A NOTARY PUBLIC*. Expect documents -- and the red sealing wax is gonna fly!

I have concealed in a traffic by-law amendment the requirement that all Toronto schoolchildren must view at least one Buster Keaton film per year.

With the imminent departure of Toronto's final hippie, we can now retire our two-man undercover hippie cop squad, The Unwashables.

I'm judging the International Children's Scat Singing Jamboree at Fort York. L'il devils can barely form sentences, so this comes naturally to them!

BREAKING: expect hailstones the size of a cheap bastard's idea of a classy engagement ring.

. . .

Labour strike at Thorncliffe Sayvette's is in its third ugly day; workers are now building tents and bonfires from Shelley Winters-brand muumuus.

My Hollywood spies say 1974's big film will be Charlton Heston's *HUEY LONG*. It will also be released in the X-rated market with a question mark at the end.

Expect fireworks today at City Council as drunken aldermen dance around an open flame while holding gunpowder.

Final straw for striking workers at Thorncliffe Sayvette's: six-hour training session on how to wear an 'Ilya Kuryakin' *MAN FROM U.N.C.L.E.* wig.

Chrome dome Yul Brynner in town today to promote his line of impassiveness pills.

Toronto is blessed to have Sick Kids Hospital, but euphemists won't allow Gents' Eruptive Boil Lancery, or Dominion Brain Puncture Suctionette.

Shuttle buses will be running between TTC Summerhill and Rosedale stations this afternoon just for something to do.

Surprise Beatles reunion as Ringo Starkey and Yoko Ono join forces to fight obscurity in Norman Jewison's *FABRIC*.

Fun Fact: John Graves Simcoe was a gaseous windbag who frequently stared at pigeons just a little too long.

Police called to scene of ointment.

I'm cutting the ribbon at the opening of Canadian Specific Limited's new Leaside factory, where opaque ant farms and novelty 11-foot poles are to be made.

Deer Park Library is now lending out false eyelashes, marriage proposals and cardboard thought bubbles.

A forgotten underground river beneath Bloor Street has surfaced at Bay St. and is swollen with treading matrons and their purses.

Join us for my Festival of Zoning! Eat, talk, loiter, slaughter cattle or count cicadas, according to your zone and social standing.

Housewives will be delighted: City of Toronto aerial hair spraying of key posh neighbourhoods resumes in time for tea party season.

I'm greeting a hovercraft delegation of Madagascarian ventriloquists, here to study our way of speaking out of both sides of our mouths.

Bayview Extension closed due to Riverdale Zoo giraffe spoor avalanche.

'Man changing trousers on subway platform' is also known as a 'George McCready' in TTC parlance.

Merely as a public service I often pose for stock photo catalogs as e.g. 'cranky barber', 'man about to sneeze', 'disgruntled spelunker', and 'crazed auctioneer'.

I'm at the Royal York Hotel's Imperial Room enduring Lucille Ball and Luci Arnaz in their out-of-sync musical revue 'Just For The L of It'.

Fired another projectionist last night, 14th so far this year. This one was shaving his back with a splicer during *PULVERIZE*. Hair in the gate? Hello!

At the Leaside Biennale, 'art' show in a laxative factory. My kid could paint better than these 'artists', but he's an idiot so he won't.

Also opening at Imperial Six today: Donald Pleasance, Suzanne Pleshette and Paul Anka in muffler repair heist pic *THE ESOPHAGUS CALCULATION*.

Fran's is serving me my favourite chocolate chip scrambled eggs just the way I like them: without judgment.

I'm in my Burt Lancaster-brand slumber slacks, opening a canned ham. Got the Perly's map out and am planning additional escape routes out of Toronto.

This weekend at Fort York: learn, or unlearn, how to make your own cannon fodder.

Secret to my success? I have dozens of ottomans stored all over the city so that when I need to put my feet up, hey presto!

Overly-concrete Robarts Library could withstand an assault from ground troops, but will inevitably crumble into a powdery mess due to the fetid, drug-laced breaths of moronic students.

. . .

Fun Fact: the population density of Rosedale during summer long weekends is about the same as the Henryk Arctowski Polish Antarctic Station.

Unveiling my proposal for Highway 402: it would run parallel to 401, but banked like a racetrack, to allow for passing at 200-300 MPH.

Apollo 23 capsule has landed in Riverdale Zoo by mistake. Astronauts are fine, and are being licked by two hyenas.

Signing copies of my new book, *CANADA DRY, REST OF WORLD GLOOMY*, now at Britnell's. As always, bring your own pen --- this ain't Red China!

Robert Redford tells me he prepared for his role as 'The Great Gatsby' by being rich.

I'm on page 814 of the celebrity 1973 Canadian Tire catalogue playfully pointing jumper cables at Neil Young. 'Get a haircut!'. Har har.

Tonite on *MANNIX*: a conman fleeces a rube, but Joe puts him in a Chicago overcoat as no one ever drips the constellation if Joe's the mop handle.

Fun Fact: 'No' is said more often in Toronto than in any other city in the Western Hemisphere.

In the new issue of General Hooray, 'the only Canadian celebrity magazine allowed', Lorne Greene admits he's never adjusted to 'talkies'.

. . .

City Hall typing pool gals swooning as Hollywood's Elliott Gould drops by for a nosh, and to identify a body in the morgue. Why do Fu Manchu moustaches have this impact on women?!

My Hollywood spies tell me 1974 will see Don Adams and Stubby Kaye in *FRENCH CONNECTION 3: EIFFEL OF TROUBLE.*

Reading Pierre Berton's magisterial history of municipal reeves, *BY-LAW OR BY CROOK.* I can't put it down, because of peer pressure.

Parliament St. isn't even pretending to try anymore.

Left off Toronto maps for decades due to cartographical myopia and surveyor alcoholism, little-known and lightly-loved Hawaiian Yonge St. is being razed today.

Opening today at the Imperial Six: Robert Stack, Robert Culp, Robert Morse and Roberta Flack in *BOBBING FOR MURDER.*

Tame tigers and shy iguanas will wander thru TTC subway trains today as a charming promotion for Metro Zoo's 'Anthropomorphic Days'.

Centre Island ferries stink of leisure.

Tonite's meeting of Undersexed Men of North Toronto was cancelled due to a lack of verve.

Let's be honest. Dupont St. and Davenport Rd. are essentially the same street.

· · ·

Yet another extremely minor British royal, Baronessette Chippy Pert, is in Toronto today to speak at inbreeding conference.

The long-overdue dry cleaning of Fort York has begun.

Annual bonfire of hair collected from Toronto barbershop floors commences at Ramsden Park at 6pm. Expect blonde embers.

My power has NOT gone to my head. It has gone directly to my hips.

Now playing at the Imperial Six: James Franciscus as Superman, Joey Heatherton as Lois Lane and Paul Lynde as Lex Luthor in *KRYPTONUTS*.

We've collected all the discarded crap from melting snowbanks --- it's now on display at the Automotive Building for pickup at your convenience.

Opening today at the Imperial Six: Gary Moore, Edith Head and Agnes Moorehead in *LLAMAS OPTIONAL*.

Reports coming in from Leaside that potato salad is no longer considered credible as a main course.

Diarrhea ain't gonna stop Geoff from becoming the world's fastest mountain climber in *BLEACHED LIGHTNING 2: DON'T LOOK UP*, opening Friday at the Imperial Six.

Toronto's last toupée farm, Combover Acres on Bayview Ave., is closing due to the fact that ladies have noticed something's off.

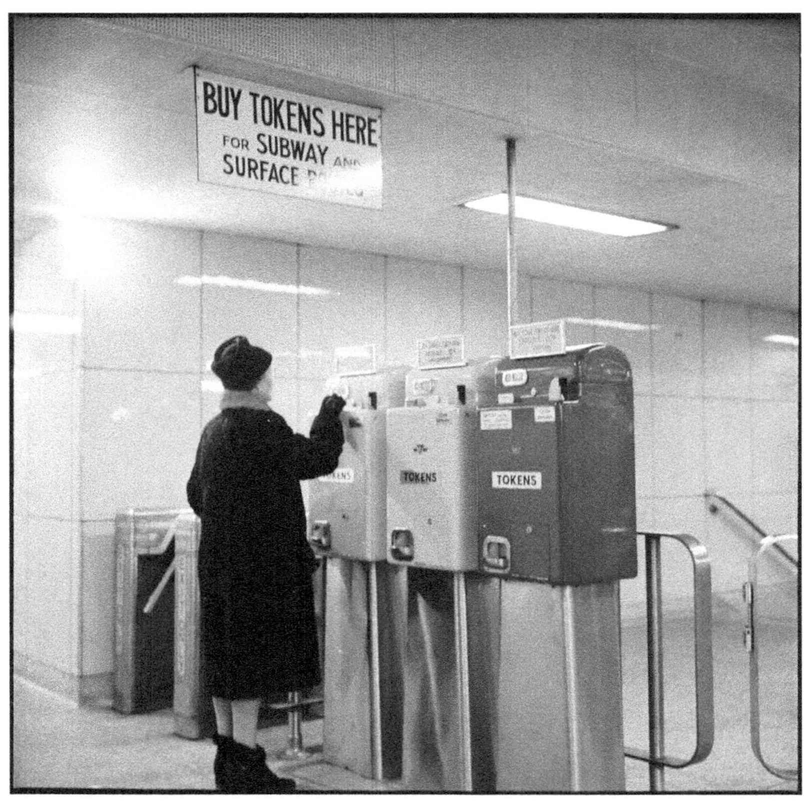

City of Toronto Archives, Fonds 1567, Series 648, File 79, Item 2

Mrs. Bernice Thrint purchases her favourite flavour of TTC token (pound cake) eschewing the adjacent potato soup and burnt Salisbury Steak flavours.

7

JUST PARKETTE IT, BUSTER

Man must exert his authority over all the beasts. Thus is it written in the Bible and, coincidentally, in the City of Toronto Noxious Weeds, Perfumes and Beasts Act of 1937.

As much as one might wish to see every square inch of a burgeoning city paved and built over with whatever a given era's equivalent of mud cake drywall or Herculean balsa wood might be, it should be acknowledged that a city cannot thrive unless its toiling workers can also catch a glimpse, or at least a peripheral whiff, of nature.

And so it behooves City authorities, of which I am the utmost, to cultivate and fertilize that which nature has left behind in order to direct citizens' attention to pasteurized pastures, so to speak—if only to distract them ever-so-briefly from the relentless din and horror of their miserable micro-eons on earth.

As stewards of the City's parks, we must adhere to certain underlying principles of urban recreational agriculture. These include: keep people vertical; throttle excessive frolicking; ensure parks are uninhabitable after 5 p.m., and stanch the flow of disintegrating picnic potato salad into the groundwater.

I can confidently assert that we are generally in adherence with these maxims, be it through the incessant and aggressively odiferous re-sodding of High Park, the off-duty truancy officers who volunteer their time to scream at prostrate book readers in Ramsden Park, the electrical amplification of cicada screeching at dullish dusk in Withrow Park, or the installation of bank vault-level security doors in Davisville Park's washrooms, too heavy for any but the most muscular or blad-der-conscious to heave open.

That having been said, we do pride ourselves on providing the most median level of natural precincts. For example, I have recently approved the installation of perhaps two, but no more than three, temporary and fully transparent wooing gazebos in City parks as an experiment in controlled outdoor human interaction.

Some have noted the deft craft of our park naming policy. Surely more people would wish to enter, say, the Headless Chicken Pot Pie Amusement and Mood Amelioration Oasis than the off-putting Comptroller and Mrs. Cecil Willoughby Memorial Parkette? So our practice of only naming parks after the most obscure and inept City bureaucrats has worked like a linguistic repellent at park gates, controlling the flow of loitering locals and unimaginative wandering tourists alike.

Speaking of parkettes, they are a Toronto invention (by me), effectively limiting the number of people who could possibly stand to be there, and making it impossible for a group to assemble a quorum for a game of old-timey Pass the Responsibility.

It might have been Dickens, or perhaps it was Dick Van Dyke, who once declared that parks are the lungs of a great city. Well, in Toronto, we rarely allow the word "great" to be thrown around. And our parks are better defined as this city's nostrils—holes to the soul best not thought about much.

City of Toronto Archives, Fonds 1128, Series 381, File 274, Item 11372-5

Notorious TTC subway fare evaders, the smooth and insolvent fraternal quadruplets, 'TNT', 'Skull', 'Shiv' and 'Aspirin' Jones, act all casual-like as they make a run for it right onto the tracks. The fines are modest, but the shame is debilitating.

❧ 8 ❧
THAT'S A LOVELY ROTUNDA
YOU HAVE THERE

GENERAL PICTURE SUBJECTS

Nothing to worry about: the purple flames and smoke rising over Fleet St. are coming from our annual dog feces bonfire.

Seventeen key downtown Toronto intersections will be blocked off today as we test some new experimental sawhorses.

· · ·

Fun Fact: 7,000 Lake Ontario trout are killed each year from mascara washed down drains of weeping wives arguing with their doofus husbands.

Tonite on *TOUPÉE COP*: Bruno Gerussi teams up with a female lady doctor (Anne Murray) to reveal the toxic materials found in ersatz toupées -- equine dental floss, navel lint, dynamite fuses, discarded Transatlantic Morse code cables, and typewriter ribbons used to write pornos.

I'm thinking of cancelling the CNE Air Show, and instead issuing free sunglasses with stencils of the Avro Arrow on the lenses.

Spring has sprung at Riverside Zoo! And with it the priapic egotism of the chimpanzees, egged on by certain elements in the fox contingent.

TTC Rosedale bus to be re-routed to snub the Eaton brothers.

When I was a cub reporter for the Leaside Extortionist in 1930, court stenographers transcribed *everything* -- every cough, door slam, eye roll, abuse of pencil erasers, socks being pulled up, wind being passed, robe fondling etc. It's where I got my love of truthful fabulation.

In Victorian Toronto there were only eleven chairs.

James Bond is back and this time he's nursing a cold, in *DEATH BREATH*, starring Anthony Newley as 007 and Oliver Reed as Potty Mouth.

Planning a vacation? Consider visiting our twin city, New Toronto, which is right over there.

. . .

Tonite on *MANNIX*: Joe finds a dead body behind a swanky nightclub and his first thought is "wow, nice shoes."

It's sentient apes day at Riverdale Zoo, but please bring exact change, as they're not *that* smart.

UNEARTHED! Ontario Audio-Visual-Temporal Censor Board's print of my 1937 film *CHICK CHESTERFIELD: TORONTO DICK: DIVORCE BY SPATULA.*

Attention City Hall staff: motivational speaker Lloyd Ronny, Top Handkerchief Salesman in 1947 and 1951 (he had a toothache in the intervening years) will be speaking at 4 p.m. on the topic 'How I Took The Snot Rag And Made It America's Must-Have Accoutrement.'

Toronto's tallest building, the 123-storey SkyLozenge, will house divorcées, errant uncles, spare tires and the offices of Thrill Gum.

Fun Fact: 'tantalizing one's neighbour', while morally reprehensible, is sexily defined and allowed under Toronto zoning bylaws.

Effective immediately, the word 'thud' and the expression 'pinch me' are not to be used in official City Hall memos.

If you are wondering why Jarvis St. looks a bit like a handsome blonde Kirk Douglas this morning, it's because Bruno Gerussi, star of the hit show *TOUPÉE COP*, has donated 1,000 ersatz prop toupées to help us fill in potholes. So drive carefully, and swerve past the dashing do's!!

TTC paper transfers will now be 3 pages long, as we are adding necessary provisos, stipulations, codicils, warnings, Catch-22's and limericks.

. . .

Most auxiliary cops in this city are plug ugly. Does this weaken their already watery authority? I'm commissioning a study.

I'm at Cannes' un-unctuous Champoo Hotel. It seems to be run by members of the French Resistance, as they're resisting all of my requests!

Top movie stars send their stunt doubles to Cannes premieres, to avoid germs. You should see 'Lee Marvin': a Turkish boxer with an addiction to Brylcreem.

Just announced here at Cannes: child's comic book hero Mr. Bruce Wayne is coming to the big screen in *BATUSI*, starring Jack Lord.

French bureaucracy here at Cannes is legendary, e.g. villains in James Bond films must be licensed to die.

I arrived here in Cannes in a Warner Bros. Chinese junk, after a bilious nite with Karen Black, Pelé and Lloyd Bochner, stars of *CHOP-STICK GUN*.

I've switched now to my favourite deluxe hotel here in Cannes, The Per Diem. The 'expense claim concierge' Gaston knows all the angles!

Here in Cannes the French pronounce 'croissant' as 'kwahsahn', like it's a secret code or something.

Cannes premiere of Jerry Lewis' Cold War opus *KOOKY KUDDLES* is in French with French subtitles, because they just won't let it go.

. . .

Delay at TTC Coxwell due to the escalator horseplay by Mrs. Gobel's Grade 5 class, especially notorious cut-ups Lester Brannigan and Bub Omerto, has now cleared.

Sales are up at Simcoe St. Goatworks by 18%! However, goats are down, in terms of motivation, demeanour, helpfulness.

Jarvis Collegiate night school course 'How To Lunge' has been cancelled tonite as the instructor has fled the country.

I'm speaking today to the World Rotunda Association on the topic 'That's A Lovely Rotunda You Have There'.

Leafs announce monster trade: Eddie Shack to the Cleveland Barons for some fine Lake Erie cottage properties.

Fun Fact: none of Toronto's top poets actually live here; they all commute into the city daily for muse reasons.

I'll be signing pairs of my exclusive line of gents' confidence-building underpants, Uprights, at Thorncliffe Sayvette's tonite.

Important Notice: Do NOT use your toaster between 10-11 a.m. as the City will be flushing out the crumb system.

Today's Soup of the Day in Toronto is Postponed Turnip.

Delay on TTC Queen streetcar due to plunging neckline.

· · ·

Opening this week at the Imperial Six: Elizabeth Taylor, Dub Taylor and Taylor Mead in Guam's last-ever gothic potboiler *CITRUS YEARNINGS*.

City hasn't time nor $$ to fill all the potholes. So we'll name 'em! The Sherbourne Orifice. The Bathurst Puncture. The Balliol Gape.

Stanley Kubrick here to scout locations for his next brainy epic *ALUMINUM COFFEE*, with Lon Chaney Jr. Jr. (sic). I shan't exhibit it.

Opening Friday at Imperial Six: Bob Crane, Lee Merriweather and Klaus Kinski as Dr. Sliver in uric acid heist pic *MONKEY SEE, MONKEY PEE*.

Join us at the Imperial Six this weekend for an alphabetically-curated retrospective of the films of Peter Lawford from *AMMO HOLIDAY* to *BACON FAT SCARS* to *CANKER*.

Roncesvalles spelled backwards is a terrible idea.

Tonite on *THE DEAN MARTIN SHOW*: Charlie Callas sings a 19th century dirge for dead whales, taking all the fun out of the show.

Tonite on *KOJAK*: Telly Savalas demands that background extras mumble his lines so he doesn't have to memorize them.

Police arrest writers for sitcom *THE TROUBLE WITH TRACY* – they're so bereft of ideas they've been breaking into homes to transcribe husband and wife arguments.

So proud that City of Toronto's first fink satellite launched into space today from Pape Ave. Spaceport. Will monitor scumbags et al.

· · ·

Every article of clothing I am wearing today is elasticized. Hence the tension.

Spending the nite posing for menu fotos for Fran's Yonge and St. Clair. Without me, the Frog's Legs Benedict would look repulsive.

Toronto is sometimes a snake eating its tail that doesn't like the taste.

I'll be in Gordon Lightfoot Ravine today with a copy of Mickey Spillane's *HIGH-CALIBRE DAMES* and a thermos of Bovril Eggnog if anyone needs me.

Opening Friday at the Imperial Six: Dr. Joyce Brothers, the Smothers Brothers, the Lennon Sisters and Moms Mabley in *SCORPION THUGS*.

No excuse is pathetic if it works.

Today in General Hooray, Canada's only domestic celebrity magazine, we ask Lloyd Bochner "when did you pay off your mortgage?"

Spooky kooky storyist J.D. Salinger in town today to get his fake beard tweaked.

Opening Friday at the Imperial Six: Richard Burton, Marty Feldman and Yvonne de Carlo in airplane food heist pic *I'M BOEING TO KILL YOU.*

Tonite I'll be at the Royal York Imperial Room to see Bette Davis tear up the scenery (i.e. Group of Seven murals) in *ANTI-MAME.*

· · ·

A round of applause for the Centre Island snack bar staff, who kept the hot dog water boiling all winter, just in case.

All Toronto-area Zumburger and Steak 'N Burger locations will be merged into one chain, Hoof 'N Mouth, as of January 1974.

Defunct comedy duo Rowan and Martin in Toronto today to discuss a merger with Wayne and Shuster.

Opening Friday at the Imperial Six: producer Irwin Allen's disasterelishing style is on-screen again in the powerfully overt pic SPRAIN!

Sometimes it feels like the monkey on my back just sneezed on my neck.

DICK CLIPS A CREEP, one of my 1940s *CHICK CHESTERFIELD: TORONTO DICK* movies, featured Yvette De Carlo, Yvonne's zaftig unicycling twin.

Seven Pape Ave. bungalows have been declared off-limits as bungalow pox spreads its hatefully shoddy humidity.

Opening tomorrow: Valerie Perrine, Dick Shawn, William Demarest and Toshiro Mifune in nail salon heist pic *THE CUTICLE PALPITATION.*

Artist with a moustache (or is it the other way around?) LeRoy Neiman is in town taping his Christmas special at CFTO-TV, *NUDE YULE*. Ugh.

· · ·

New at the Imperial Six's experimental concession stand: cabbage wafers, liver cider and gravy volcanoes. Try a flagon of bug nog!!

300 Toronto dry cleaners meeting today at the Northrop Frye Motor Hotel to reach agreement on how needlessly repetitive it all is.

Catching Buddy Ebsen's cabaret tribute to hearsay, *RUMOUR TUMOUR* at the Bayview Playhouse. Lots of empty seats, but that adds to the drama.

Now at Aikenhead's: decorative cardboard privacy shields so drunks who wet their pants can saunter home, not scuttle.

Ticketed and towed this morning: Mr. Reginald Toomey's 1970 Dodge Consequences, seen with a festering glove compartment; Mrs. Dolly Bixby's 1955 Oldsmobile Shirk, idling with intent; and a Pape Ave. Doll Hospital ambulance.

Police called to Senator Q. Archie Prufrock Medical-Dental-Sexual Building at St. George and Bloor.

Need to borrow a paper clip? Branches of the Toronto Public Library offer short-term loans of 3-5 paper clips so that your papers don't scatter hither and thither, mussing up the city during these difficult times.

Why not impugn your palate tonite at Tony Ontario's Are You Going To Finish That? Restaurantorium, serving the finest food barely-touched by celebrities! We'll never know why Pierre Berton didn't (or couldn't?) finish that volcano of rice pudding, but some things are best left.

· · ·

Fun Fact: In Victorian Toronto, every day was Victoria Day, but some days were more Victorian than others.

Having drinks high atop Bulova Tower with Robert Goulet who is now throwing dozens of cologne bottles over the railing in his annual cleansing.

When the Imperial Six's ceremonial red carpet was sent out for cleaning, they drained 15 gallons of cola syrup from it, and six teeth.

Beefy thespian Raymond Burr in town shooting a pilot for a *PERRY MASON* spin-off, *PERRY MASON'S FOOD COURT*, "where justice comes well done".

In Victorian Toronto, some folks still had erotic dreams about John Graves Simcoe.

A single TTC token gets you a ticket to 1p.m. showing of Peter Lawford's *PULVERIZE*! He's related to the Kennedys, so you know it's good!

Tripod industry in Toronto is growing, but needs more things to put on top of the tripods. So far, vegetables, logs and small pets have been ineffective.

City of Toronto Archives, Fonds 1567, Series 648, File 133, Item 21

The TTC is introducing separate subway entrances and exits for divorcing couples, to reduce platform bickering, turnstile recriminations and transfer machine blame.

❧ *9* ☙

WHERE MATH TAKES A BATH

THE CITY'S BUDGET

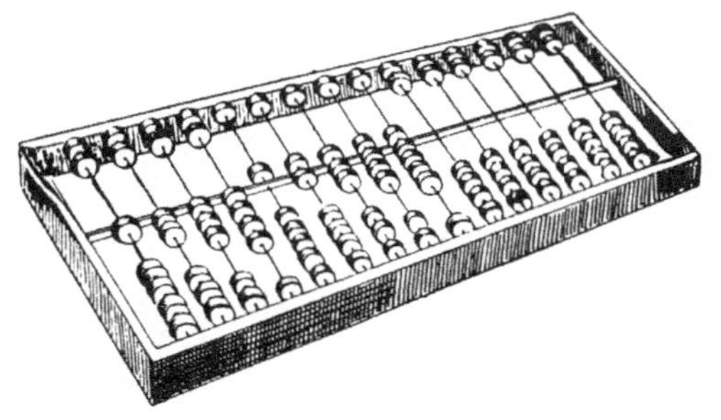

The exact circumference of Telly Savalas' head. The correct pronunciation of the word 'tchotchke'. How a grape knows which kind of wine to become. Why no one can say 'alabaster' without smirking. These and other mysteries may have plagued mankind for millennia or moments, but they pale in comparison to the septic stench of fiscal confusion that is the City of Toronto's finances.

From comptrollers to con men, from accountants to real estate touts, from \$ to ?, how and how much money the City gathers, records, disguises, disperses, and moans about has defied human understanding, until now. As your mayor, it is my job to understand the blood

77

(revenue), as well as the bile (expenditures). Money in, money out, but along the way, it's E=MC2 meets Hieronymus Bosch. Let me try to explain it all to you.

A slovenly bub's bungalow or a rich bastard's ego-acre, it matters not. Everyone pays property tax, which generates the largest and most mouth-watering share of the City's income. Property assessment is based on an age-old formula: square footage + eavestrough heft x street snootiness ratio + annual number of toilet flushes = your tax bill. It may not make sense, but it does make money.

Businesses and industrial concerns, from the Grand Trunk Railroad Shirt Cardboard Co., to the Pape Avenue Phrenology Clinic, and from the salamander oozeries to the Parcheesi parlours that line Toronto's carefree crescents and puckish promenades—all pay the City a flat $428.17 per annum, which seems fair, now that I think about it.

Once the money arrives from citizen or corporation at the Dufferin Street Counting and Skimming Pavilion (at it does in crumpled bills, greasy cheques, and teeth-marked silver dollars), it is cleaned, sorted, fondled, and ooh-ed over for several days. Then, and only then, are the funds counted by a squad of angry Scottish schoolmarms, the most trustworthy and ruthless in the land.

The final tally is written in chalk, as was done in ancient times, on the back wall of City Hall, where it is photographed, and mulled over for several weeks. At last, the august body known as the Toronto Sinking Fund Secretariat meets over roast beef sandwiches to divvy it all up.

Cops' billy clubs, streetcar track lubrication, the hydrant laureate's office, and the Works Department employees' attendance at the annual World Asphalt Auction in Montenegro account for somewhere between three and 68 per cent of our annual expenditures, depending on exchange rates and the vagaries of nepotism.

. . .

With the little that's left over, we have to keep Toronto humming as reliably as a Leafs fan during the third stanza of 'O Canada'. Have we succeeded in managing this great metropolis' ebbs and flows? Only time, and the efforts of exceedingly bored archeologists in the year 2173, will be able to answer that question. As for the taxation system itself, could it be better? Fairer? Less reliant on abacuses? Sure. But just as your pancreas might greatly benefit from a bit of sunlight and a thorough scrubbing, you really don't want to open things up to make that happen.

City of Toronto Archives Fonds 200, Series 372, Subseries 1, Item 1428

Toronto's first-ever box park opens June 1!! Children who are sliver-prone should proceed as usual to the Davisville Ave. Jello Park.

WORLD'S LARGEST
ANNULMENT CEREMONY

I suspect there has been widespread cheating on the Imperial Six ushers' entry exam. How could they ALL know that Otto Preminger is a prick?

Elevator Operators Union is working to rule today, refusing to hand out lyrics for the Muzak selections.

Congratulations to City Hall's Sod Department for being the world's first government dept. to successfully create an octuplicate requisition form, i.e. one with eight carbon copies. 'Press hard', as I like to say!

· · ·

Beat the heat with a frothy broth of non-hot cow contents at Pape Avenue's beloved Post-War Milkshakes Pavilion, featuring World Trade Organization-compliant flavours such as Triplicate Saltpetre, Caucasian Vanilla, Hospital Cafeteria Beige, Pleated Poundcake, Factory Issue or Gelatin Powder Filler.

Typewriter Repairmen's Union party has spilled into the streets, its drunks shouting "@#$%&!".

I'm guest host today at noon on CBC Radio's beloved medical call-in show *We'll Talk You Through Your Charley Horse*.

We welcome these new themed floats to the Dominion Day Parade: Milk of Magnesia, Old Ed's Salisbury Steak, TTC Rail-Grinding Car.

Toronto's last bespoke grappling hook store, Pape Vertical Aids and Such, closes its doors this week, a victim of changing social mores.

Centre Island summer jobs available: Barnacle Pointer; Flume Ride Guinea Pig; Ferry Explainer; Puppet Theatre Bouncer; Llamaturge.

Our first 'Fishing For Compliments' booth opens today at TTC Chester station. Staffed with sycophants and featuring flattering lighting.

Fortified for the day ahead with a Lee Marvin 'Dirty Dozen' breakfast: a dozen eggs and one plucky chicken, cooked with the odds against them.

Fun Fact: in Victorian Toronto, only the Lieutenant-Governor was allowed to gaze upon margarine.

. . .

A mysterious bulging package prompts wetness in the barely erotic French thriller *THE CROTCH OF AIX*, opening Friday at the Imperial Six.

Join us at City Hall for Dominion Day Distractions, including the Kidz Re-Zone, Pin The Tail on the Gestetner Machine, Tug of Boer War, Guess Your Width Booth, and the Overdue Library Book Fines Kangaroo Court.

Some Imperial Six patrons are loosening their shirts or blouses to stay cool during this Mephistophelean heat. May I remind you that clothing, like liquor stores, is only to be opened at inconvenient times.

Tonite on *MANNIX*: Joe encounters a sexy blonde safecracker who offers to 4-35-57 him.

I'm off to the Urinal Puck Convention in Sheboygan this weekend. Between the Imperial Six and the 895 bathrooms under the City's jurisdiction, I'm the biggest buyer of these penis-focusing, odormurdering slabettes in North America. New this year: pucks signed by Bobby Orr!!

Coming to the CNE in August: World's Largest Marriage Annulment Ceremony, sponsored by Brylcreem; Bell Bottoms Exorcisms; Lyle Waggoner Takes A Stab At It; Milt Gulp's Hi-Speed Glove Compartment Emptiers; Large Pile of Turnips.

Haven't finished your last-minute Simcoe Day gift shopping? Panic not, as Sayvette's Thorncliffe is emptying its crawlspace of William Lyon Mackenzie King cigar humidor disinfectant caddies, just thirty cents, in honour of the Dirty Thirties, and King's look-the-other-way reign.

· · ·

I've been asked by CFTO-TV to help them develop a Toronto version of the geometrically sassy gameshow *HOLLYWOOD SQUARES*. So far all I've got is *LEASIDE DODECAHEDRONS*, with Lubor J. Zink, Anne Murray and Punch Imlach sulking at a picnic table.

Hollywood pulls out all the stops but cauterizes the resultant wounds in the medical extravaganza that will have you unresponsive with feelings: *SEVEN APPENDECTOMIES FOR SEVEN BROTHERS-IN-LAW*, opening Friday at the Imperial Six.

I was the first man to conceive and wear a 9-piece suit, a toupée hood and knee tassels being among the features.

Still looking for that perfect Father's Day gift for your hard-to-please goat-hating father? Consider a gift certificate from Simcoe St. Goatworks. Can be redeemed for a tour of the slaughterhouse or a goatskin hanky.

City Council voting today whether to split hairs.

Delay on TTC Mt. Pleasant streetcar as no one is taking responsibility for the tangerine rolling back and forth.

"A lot of things happen on chesterfields, but death shouldn't be one of them." Me, as Chick Chesterfield, Toronto Dick in pic *BOWLING ALLEY BLOWHARD*.

Due to extreme humidity, today's Grade 2 Smelling Bee has been cancelled.

City of Toronto is hosting an Ugly Duckling Dance for spinsters and hopeless bachelors, as we'll need more taxpayers in 20 years.

· · ·

Tonite on *BANACEK*: Banacek ponders whether adding an 'h' between the 'c' and 'e' in his name would make life a lot simpler.

Hmm. Just noticed that the official coat of arms for the City of Toronto contains the small figure of a man hesitating.

The jetpack from James Bond's *FROM RUSSIA WITH LOVE* won't be at the CNE Air Show. But the three lead crows in Hitchcock's *THE BIRDS* will be on the Food Building roof eerily cawing!

Lithe lothario Burt Reynolds in town today to promote his new 'Going Up?' line of men's elevator shoes.

ATTENTION TTC PASSENGERS: you may experience longer than normal waiting times for service. Could be decades.

Opening tomorrow at the Imperial Six: Eddie Albert is covered with measles and itching for revenge in *OINTMENT FOR MURDER*.

Last nite on *IRONSIDE*: Ironside challenged a suspect to a 45-minute staring contest. So you didn't really miss anything.

Delay on TTC Yonge line due to the sins of the fathers.

Fun Fact: the brass knuckles used by my Imperial Six ushers to subdue unruly patrons are molded from Lee Marvin's actual knuckles.

I'm ordering the grounding of all hot air balloons currently aloft over Toronto as I hate anyone looking over my shoulder.

Etobicoke closed tomorrow to re-think its raison d'être.

. . .

The high-rise apartment building at 111 Davisville Ave. has now been re-zoned as 'party central'.

Toronto's last donkey-powered ladies unmentionables factory is closing. Once the filth is cleared a mule-powered pudding shop will open in its stead.

My Hollywood spies tell me Don Knotts will go totally nude in Roman Polanski's 1974 release *ATLAS SHRUGGED*.

Police called to Don River near Bloor --- Pierre Berton has been spotted making love in a canoe. At least that's what he called it. Some shots fired.

Greeting legendary terrazzo-soprano Marjorie Plodgeworth here for her concert at the Canadian Tire Lyceum. She prefers to sing lying down.

The delay at Bathurst station due to a German tourist wearing sandals and socks caught in the escalator (code 207 or a 'Von Trapp') has now cleared.

Boatload of Bermudan immigrants is now docking at foot of Yonge St. I'm there with complimentary processed cheese slices and a big hey you.

Tonite on *THE ODD COUPLE*: Maggots make for unusual houseguests after Oscar leaves a lasagna out for three months.

. . .

Tonite on *MARCUS WELBY, M.D.*: Dr. Welby is out of his depth when pimply teen Geoff tells him he's worried about his 'lower torso feelings'.

Tonite on *HERE'S LUCY*: Mr. Mooney blows a gasket when Lucy approves some off-shore loans to a violent gang of Yakuza killers.

Tonite on *KOJAK*: Telly whips out his savalas and the network switchboard lights up.

Tonite on *MANNIX*: when confronted by a gun-wielding diamond thief, Joe doesn't flinch, though he does wet himself just a little bit.

City Hall cafeteria offerings sank to a new low this morning, e.g. a mason jar of white paste with a dollop of lard and a sprig of liver.

COMB OVER BROADWAY, the all-toupée musical some people are talking about, is back for a court-ordered run. 'Rearrange the passion!!'

This city's nudists never understand that their incessant lobbying for more shrubbery will fail as long as they lobby me while in the nude.

Having a laff with TV's Jack Webb backstage at The Colonnade prior to his one-man show *ELEANOR, WE THOROUGHLY KNEW YE*.

Gotcha! Nabbed doofus TTC driver on empty Pape bus in his stocking feet, boiling a pot of spaghetti and singing a vile sea shanty. Ignominy!

. . .

Sometimes I think Toronto taxi drivers can't tell the difference between north and south, the two Darrens on *BEWITCHED*, or right and wrong.

My Hollywood spies tell me Steve McQueen has a wooden leg -- and a personality to match!

TV's host of last resort, Ed Sullivan, in town promoting his new line of shirt cardboard, Stiff Ones.

PULVERIZE star Peter Lawford landing today at Malton in his own DC-3, 'God's Cufflinks'. He's here to dub *PULVERIZE 2: IT'S TIME TO EVISCERATE* into Cockney rhyming slang.

A naked swim in the Don River, a private screening of *STALAG 17*, the drafting of six sewage bylaws, noshing on two Franburgers and a chilled glass of Wink: my daily rite!

Hippies' Nude Tire Swing in High Park closed for maintenance.

In Victorian Toronto, the drafting of zoning bylaws was driven mostly by hate and allergies.

How busy am I? I butter my toast in advance, then freeze it the night before.

My Hollywood spies tell me Richard Dreyfuss has agreed to play the villain Grilled Cheese in 1974 James Bond pic *DIE YESTER-MORROW*, with U.K. drum-man Keith Moon as 007.

· · ·

Projectionists' Disease is sweeping thru the Imperial Six. Symptoms: lack of focus, weak story arc, and vomiting at 1:30, 3:45, 5:33, 7:50 and 9:25 p.m.

I need a bevy of something right about now.

Delay on TTC Queen streetcar as transfer chewed by passenger is flattened, dried, re-constructed and analyzed to prove validity.

Half the men in Toronto are barely half the man I am. You do the math.

Noshing on Eggs Lenny -- eggs from chickens descended from chickens owned by people mocked by Lenny Bruce.

Toronto taxi drivers must now exclude these topics from small talk with passengers: pantyhose, butter as a salve, Satan, and usury.

Dom DeLuise in town today to get out of character.

Dropped by Lichtman's to pick up Hourly Variety magazine -- I love seeing the minute-by-minute box office grosses report from Des Moines.

Eaton's truck full of Caligula soup tureens has crashed. No injuries, but the dimwitted Eaton brothers will starve tonite.

Police called to a #227, which is a prime number.

Delays this week at TTC Queen station to adjust turnstiles, as the average Toronto man's crotch has dropped noticeably since 1962.

. . .

Kibitzing at the new library branch on Centre Island, dedicated to egghead bookman Robertson Davies, who will groom his beard here from 2-3 p.m.

Whenever I have to battle the imperious Ontario government, I simply shut off the water to Queen's Park and schedule a Riverdale Zoo giraffe diarrhea clinic on Wellesley St. behind the legislature.

I am opposed to the kaleidoscope, as it is not a story medium, and so distracts youngsters from the works of, say, Billy Wilder.

Ethel Merman is in town today to bury some wigs.

Fun Fact: there is one chipmunk for every two people in Toronto, and he is exhausted.

I'm only one man. But I do have 53 salacious neckties.

Tonite on *IRONSIDE*: Raymond Burr's young brother Barney guest-stars as a master criminal who hates Raymond Burr.

Eaton's now selling tiny caskets for mashed potatoes that have grown as cold as death itself.

I'll be in my Fortress of Lassitude until Monday.

City of Toronto Archives, Fonds 200, Series 372, Subseries 10, Item 827

Bloor Viaduct Chief Engineer 'Pep' Adanac
experiences a brief moment of existential sadness as he realizes that
someday men will traverse this mighty structure solely for the purpose
of having their nose hairs trimmed on The Danforth.

THE DOMINION NUDIE ZOOPRAXOGRAPHICAL HALL

YOU'LL KISS ME WHEN I'M DONE WITH TORONTO ISLAND PARK

We have, in this marvellous City of Toronto, a public asset so magnificent in its nascent potential, so well-meaning in its character, so narcotic in its ability to entice people to lie down, that it has no international rival, save for those cities that also have islands.

I am speaking, of course, of the Toronto Island Park, more commonly known in local parlance as 'the Island' (Toronto being still admirably spartan in its civic monikers, e.g. 'the Museum' and 'the Art Gallery'). I think all right-thinking men would agree with me when I say, as I am now doing, that despite the fond position the Island holds in the bosoms of Torontonians, it is in sore need of a galvanizing and sexy re-do.

. . .

When I was a lad in the 1920's, the Island was what one might imagine as the horticultural love child of Frederick Law Olmsted and Mae West, a fantastical floating lawn of entertainment and class warfare, of sand and sermons, of hypnotic British patriotism and brazen burlesque outbursts.

All that could be eaten or drunk, from racoon-on-a-stick to Boer Lemonade, was there for the buying, along with the enticements of a cinema (my Uncle Charlie's Dominion Nudie Zoopraxographical Hall), the Moldavian Labourers' Offal Pitch, the Redundant Circuit Promenade and the controversial Co-Minglers Ankle Bath. On any given steamy August Saturday in those times, the only Torontonians NOT on the Island were the jailed, the veiled and the failed.

I won't deny that it also throbbed with a heady maritime sexual power. Fortunately, the throbbing was obscured by Christian fabrics and well-positioned shrubbery. But with the depravations of the Great Depression, many of the Island's enticements were shuttered, and with the onset of WWII, even the venerable Viceroy Felix Napping Hotel was torn down for firewood, after serving nobly as an espionage/finishing school for seducers and seductresses of Nazis.

With post-war peace came the park bureaucrats, men with a distaste for disorder, men who spent no time outdoors themselves, but who felt that those who did should do so in a barren landscape, the better to be supervised when at leisure. I must admit I was once one of those men. And so the Island was bulldozed and landscaped into a green tabula rasa, a 'there' that once one got to it was such a blindingly obvious place that the only thing to do was to immediately line up for the next ferry returning to the mainland.

We see the results today: windswept and cheerless picnics, Sahara-like stretches of bleached grass that fry the brain, inconsolable children drifting miserably inside macabre giant plastic swans, and tyrannical rule by spitefully incontinent Canada Geese. I can no longer stand idly by, watching as I do with my slightly-singed Manhattan Project binoculars, as the stolid ferries trundle back and forth across the harbour with a monotony not unlike the tedious journeys of 19th century prison ships on their way to Australia, the main difference being the presence these days of sun-burnt children wearing Batman bathing trunks.

I have a vision of the Centre Island of the future, a vision so powerful and clear that it came to me with a searing pain in my temple, a small amount of bile in my throat, and a complete set of landscape architecture blueprints in my brain.

Think skeet shooting with Jello-filled skeets.　Think nightly reenactments of the parting of the Red Sea, narrated by Paul Anka. Think toothless freshwater sharks.　Think artificial spelunking. Think barbecued steaks so thick you'd trip over them. Think an archipelago of islands of delight so enticing that Venice (Italy) will hang its excessively pomaded head in shame.

I have assembled a group of top men to put forward my plan, and, firstly, to build a meticulously-detailed maquette so life-like and compelling as to render impotent any of my political opponents (so to speak).　We'll draw on the greatest minds the world has to offer, from Butlin's Holiday Camps, to NASA, to Kresge's, and you'll begin to see what can be! We'll complete the work in time for Dominion Day in 1975.

What can a visitor expect on that glorious day? You'll arrive at the newly re-designed ferry docks, made to resemble the space station from *2001: A SPACE ODYSSEY*.　There, after a jaunty time spent being interviewed by Liquor Control Board employees, you'll be escorted on board one of our mammoth canoes (I'm talking 400-seaters, with on-board washrooms and Fran's luncheon counters) and paddled to paradise!

∙　∙　∙

Upon arrival at Centre Island, you will stare, slack-jawed in wonder, at the Plaza of The Snack Bars – and its most bejewelled establishment, Lady Eaton's Fort Pork, where all manner of cuisine, including hot dogs, wieners, franks, frankfurters, sausages and tube steaks, will be piled high. Sated, you can then waddle or be wheeled to the Western Hemisphere's largest pine tree maze, three acres of coniferous confusion, designed to mimic the hallways of City Hall's own beloved Department of Human Resources. Or cool off in our million-gallon wading pool, shaped like that almost-Great Lake, Lake St. Clair. (But wear your goggles! Chlorine levels will be at DEFCON 3, or yellow, to offset children's inevitable urine).

The current 'residents' of Ward's Island, who I am sure simply missed the final ferry of the night, will be gently whisked to higher ground, i.e. Barrie, to allow for the demolition of their rustic tarpaper shacks, and the erection of the world's only Fathers of Confederation-themed tetherball court.

A human pyramid training school, a suntan lotion sluicing pit, a 1000-seat slide projector theatre, a charades stadium — all this will be yours, dear people of Toronto, and so much more. Foreigners will flock here as well, their journey eased by the extension of the Island Airport runway through the soon-to-be-former Hanlan's Point beach to allow for landings, and attempted landings, by top-notch Boeing 747 Jumbo Jets!

How will I/you pay for all of this? In the fullness of time. The cost? No man can say. But hey! No man is an island! These things cost cash money, kiddo!

City of Toronto Archives, Fonds 1034, Item 666

My saintly mother had one of these stoves shipped to her when she was a stenographer/aviatrix/showgirl in Yonkers, New York. 'Miss Canada' was a popular appliance brand made solely for homesick expatriates.

ASEXUAL WINDOW WASHERS GUILD

Loudest fireworks explosions in Toronto tonite: Liz 'n Dick's Final Divorce, Nuclear Rice Pudding, Methuselah's Orgasm.

He-Man-nificent Peter Lawford will be at the Imperial Six tonite to check the focus on prints of his latest plot-bereft, wound-laden actioner *DISAGREEABLE FORTNIGHT*. He's such a perfectionist, except when it comes to his career.

Police called to foregone conclusion.

· · ·

Toronto's final hippie found loafing in a tree, so he's been sprayed with Hai Karate cologne, given a bologna sandwich and escorted to the Leaside border.

As it must to all men, death came today to former Toronto Mayor Elgar Perch. He will be missed, misplaced, forgotten, recalled and footnoted.

Special **TTC** shuttle bus service operating today to collect kids too stupid to get on the subway with rest of their school field trip classes.

Ontario Place Forum struggles through its 1973 season with The Captain Sans Tennille; Crosby, Stijl, Gnash and Jung; and the Boston Pips Orchestra.

For those of you at St. Andrew subway station: I knew Andrew personally and let me tell you, he was no saint.

Centre Island ferries delayed today as they are weighed down with expectations of fun that the Island cannot possibly deliver.

Gardiner Expressway ramps at Spadina and Bay closed due to bikini wax spill.

Just learned the hard way: never use the words 'moot' or 'eviscerate' in a birthday card.

Danger has a name, and it starts with M, as its name is Myrtle, in *THE POUND CAKE HAS ITS REASONS*, starring Tony Franciosa and Thelma Ritter, opening Friday at the Imperial Six.

Lorne Greene in town to narrate a divorce.

.   .   .

Tonite on *MANNIX*: Joe pretends to be a pickpocket, but mostly because he needs change for a twenty.

In an act of contrition today, all TTC Dufferin buses will drive backwards on the route to pick up the people they sped past yesterday.

This city desperately needs more hoopla.

City of Toronto drinking water may be slightly crunchy today. This is only a test.

Toronto police have discovered that ventriloquist throat lozenges, when offered to recalcitrant suspects, can increase snitching by 14%.

My surprise inspection of TTC bus drivers' fingernails has not gone well. Found under their nails: jail cell paint; dice; passengers' hair.

Today's matinee screening of cartilage comedy *ELBOW GREASE* has attracted 36 weary Fuller Brush salesmen, whose boxes of earlobe brushes are taking up seats!

You can't get decent brimstone in this town anymore.

The store for plainclothes cops, Plain & Officious, is closing. Cops will have to get suspect-resistant fedoras at Consumer's Distributing!

It's a race against the clock: Morey Amsterdam and Laurence Olivier must find new uses for cardboard or die in *IT'S CORRUGATED* at the Imperial Six.

.   .   .

Tonite on *MANNIX*: Joe adds salt to his meal.

Tomorrow's Soup of the Day is Bygone Beef.

If your window washer is not certified by the Toronto Asexual Window Washers Guild, you could be in for leering!

All-talk opera *AGNEW IN BERMUDA* is at the O'Keefe Centre, with alternate-alto Chip Thrust in the lead and Robert Goulet as a laryngitic Nixon.

No one lances boils in Karl Malden's Poughkeepsie without paying him a bribe -- it's *A TOWN WITHOUT PUS*, now playing at the Imperial Six.

The delay at TTC Osgoode station doesn't really matter, in the grand sweep of history.

Tonite on *MANNIX*: a flashback to last week's episode inadvertently includes a flash forward to this point in this week's episode.

A typewriter ribbon shortage means only one man can neatly type erotica in *DIRTY QWERTY*, starring Sonny Bono, Friday at the Imperial Six.

The Leafs have focused on the Cleveland Barons' greatest weakness in this series: their fear of public speaking.

Man-god Peter Lawford is back in town to audition scintillating ladies for his upcoming aftershave heist motion picture *THE TESTOS-TERONE OMBUDSMAN*.

· · ·

Police arrest con artist in 17-Card Monte scam, but charges dropped as potential victims nodded off due to boredom.

Today's Soup of the Day in Toronto is Oxtail Incident.

Rarely used, the TTC bus driver formal dress uniform comes with a sash, a sabre, hip waders, a periscopic helmet and a basket of fruit.

CBC Radio's long-running soap opera, *'Moisten The Canadian Shield'*, ends tonite as Wilma parachutes to freedom from Sudbury's Big Nickel.

Riverdale Zoo closed this weekend to allow the hyenas to take things down a notch.

Hell hath no fury but it does have a lovely tush in *SATAN'S BUTTOCKS*, starring Desi Arnaz and Pam Grier, opening Friday at the Imperial Six.

Tonite on *IRONSIDE*: to hide the fact that Raymond Burr uses cue cards, the rest of the cast looks in the same direction as if it's a sunset.

April may be the cruelest month, but 3:30 a.m. is a real asshole.

Failure packs a wallop, and a quart of lime rickey in *HAVEN'T YOU DONE ENOUGH?* starring Michael Landon and Martha Raye, at the Imperial Six.

Today's Soup of the Day in Toronto is Throbbing Minestrone.

· · ·

I've asked police detectives, when dusting for fingerprints at a crime scene, to do the rest of the dusting, primp the pillows etc.

In today's City of Toronto Zoning Department crossword puzzle, the correct answer to 37 down is 'placate'.

Delay on TTC Mt. Pleasant streetcar at the cemetery, as the sins of the father, etc. etc.

Those who forget history are doomed to forget that Prime Minister Louis St. Laurent had lovely eyes.

I'm very good at thwarting.

Toronto is the world's leading producer of flavoured wax lips, providing 77% of the globe's needs and 850% of its wants for this product.

At the CNE Air Show: *BONANZA* star Dan Blocker will be kept aloft for 20 minutes by 127 industrial-strength hand blow-dryers.

Watch my *CHICK CHESTERFIELD: TORONTO DICK* films carefully and you'll notice I never blink --- it's my subtle tribute to ophthalmologists.

I'm back in the Canadian Tire catalog! Page 547, nude except for a Group of Seven-themed stick shift cover.

City Hall cafeteria now offering all meals in lozenge form, to save space. Try the lozagna!!

.   .   .

Lombard St. closed today for the City Morgue's annual staff picnic, Informaldehyde.

Have you picked up your complimentary City of Toronto anti-cicada earplugs yet? I know I have!

Lee J. Cobb in town today to berate the first person he sees.

Men with sandals are advised to stay indoors today. Or pretty much every day.

Coming to the CNE next month: George Theb's Hi-Speed Parallel Parkers, Wayne and Shuster's *WHO'S AFRAID OF VIRGINIA WOOLF?*, and the RCMP Medical Ride.

Be alarmed not, dear citizens. The electric eels in the Don River are placed there to deter nudists, gold panners and illegal launderers.

Adventure has a name, and it's unpronounceable in *THE SCAPEGOAT DEFIBRILLATION*, coming soon to the Imperial Six.

It'll keep you alive or kill you dead. Robert Vaughan takes on *THE VITAMIN VOLCANO*, now at the Imperial Six.

I'm no miracle worker, though Buddy Ebsen's career might disagree.

I'm banning mezzanines in Toronto buildings, as no one knows what they are.

· · ·

Peter Lawford Film Festival tomorrow at the Imperial Six includes *A LADY BUT FOR THE PENIS, CUFFLINKS SLAUGHTER*, and *SOUL DRAIN*.

The crowd here at Fran's at Yonge and St. Clair is getting ugly fast, which is something, seeing as they were already ghastly when they came in.

I've lobbied for years to have the International Dateline moved to Toronto to help sex this city up.

Tonite on *BARNABY JONES*: Barnaby is too tired to interrogate a robbery suspect, so sends his false teeth instead.

Coming to the CNE: the children of The Three Stooges open up about their dads' comedic concussions, headaches and hair loss.

You may experience longer than normal delays on the TTC Yonge line. Or, you may choose to forget them, and think of lilacs.

Tonite on *MANNIX*: Joe confuses a safecracker by shouting out random numbers.

Tonite on *KOJAK*: a young cop loses his virginity to a turnstile and won't shut up about it.

Scientists tell me dinosaurs once strode mightily across Toronto's verdant precincts, but they stunk up the joint.

My advice to shiftless teenagers: your pimples aren't going to pop themselves, but I've been wrong before.

· · ·

All Toronto escalators will be still tomorrow for one hour, to get your fat ass moving and shed this city a few pounds.

It's Tony Curtis week here at the Imperial Six! Free admission to those who have changed their names, or bathed Laurence Olivier.

Fun Fact: ballot boxes used in our recent municipal vote will now serve as ottomans for trusted stool pigeons at the Don Jail.

Mrs. Xanadu has me on an all-placebo diet. Or so she says.

There is no 'I' in team, but there's usually one smug bastard.

Robert Goulet in town this weekend to meet with his goatee coach.

Centerville Log Flume ride closed today for refluming.

New popularity poll has me at 84%, Ghost of Christmas Past at 7%, an old rolled-up newspaper at 6%, that mouse in your cupboard at 3%.

The children of this city need more walkie-talkies.

'Re-Elect Mayor Bert Xanadu' lawn signs are now available in these sizes: Shy, Bold, Cult-ish, Gibraltar, and Visible From Outer Space.

I was once re-elected while holed up in a Monte Carlo casino, playing craps. I've tried to govern Toronto that way ever since.

· · ·

New features at Cement Truck Drivers' Lounge on Gerrard St. include caramel foot bath, excuses swap box, and the eternal vat of chili.

Stay indoors tonite - incinerators will be burning off the hate mail and deliberately-spoiled meat sent to City Council.

Traffic on Mt. Pleasant Rd. is moving, but just not fast enough to be perceived by humans.

In Victorian Toronto no one hurried, as if they somehow knew that the result of their labours would only result in us.

Fun Fact: the design of the U-shaped rows of aldermen's seats in the Council chamber are based on the dentures of our first three mayors.

In this issue of General Hooray, Canada's Sole Remaining Celebrity Magazine, we discuss the quiet satisfaction of anonymity.

Police called to a friendship-ending fondue.

The sands of time have found their way into my undershorts.

High humidity is making TTC Bathurst station uncomfortably sexy.

The starry twinkling in the sky over Toronto tonite is just a scheduled urine dump from Soviet spacecraft Smegma 7.

City of Toronto Archives, Fonds 220, Series 65, File 100, Item 47

Members of the popular rumba band The Shirtless Walters stretch their limbs and our credulity amidst the hedges outside the city's only nightclub where coat hangers are banned and shimmying is mandatory.

THE SULLEN THROCKMORTON
OCTUPLETS

You can tell that the CNE will open soon: I just signed the permit for the Annual Open-Air Washing of the Carnies.

Opening Friday at the Imperial Six: Peter Lawford tells the Mafia where to get off in the plasma-curdling thriller *ELEVATOR OPER-ATOR ASSASSIN.*

Ticketed and towed today: Mr. Benny Spral's 1952 Chrysler Anvil, left in neutral with the radio playing atonal jazz; a bus from the Pape Ave.

Marionette College, leaking sandwich spread; a Boer War-themed bumper car illegally made roadworthy.

TTC's All-Nude Streetcar service to Hanlan's Point ferry docks officially a failure, say dermatologists.

Tonite on *KOJAK*: there are red faces all around as Kojak's ties to Greece's fascist government are revealed.

Chronic shortage of slacks explains why three men have been spotted on Dufferin St. wearing grass hula skirts. Or perhaps it doesn't.

Meet the sullen Throckmorton Octuplets at the CNE! They water ski, yodel and bicker to a funereal soundtrack!

A grim phalanx of City eavestrough inspectors will be sweeping across Toronto today. However, due to wet and slippery conditions, they'll just take your word for it.

Tonite on *MANNIX*: Joe sweet talks his way into a bar that only serves court stenographers, and then has to sweet mime his way back out.

I can only describe my current chocolate eclair as 'palatial', simply because arcane city council rules forbid me from describing it as 'Brobdingnagian'.

Imperial Six's Theatre 5 will be closed this afternoon as we install corn-on-the-cob caddies at each seat for tonite's opening of the Lee Marvin/Dom DeLuise Uruguayan notary public thriller *BUTTERED DEATH*.

· · ·

Toronto wading pools have passed gazpacho temperatures, now approaching broth, will be shut down at crème brûlée.

Wonderful to see Mr. Magoo is finally off the Hollywood blacklist!!

Most of Toronto is currently draining into a pothole on Pape.

The TTC is offering free copies of Arthur Hailey's new potboiler *UPHOLSTERY!* and fist-shaped pastries and that you can save in waxed paper for sustenance during the next subway delay.

I'm told that when it is completed in 1976, the CN Tower will sway in the wind, much like a tipsy Charles de Gaulle.

Opening Toronto's thinnest parkette today on Bay St. Its only purpose: a place for men to stop to re-tie their loose shoelaces.

Fun Fact: the Ontario Censor Board now also has jurisdiction over public sexual euphemisms. Wait till they hear about Honey Dew Restaurants.

Don't forget to renew your stepladder licence. Comes with wax seal of verification, usage diary, neighbour-shooing stick, and altimeter.

I'm more of glass half-Scotch kind of person.

In one of my *CHICK CHESTERFIELD: TORONTO DICK* pics, *DEATH COMES IN GALLONS*, I thwart a hootched-up dentist's plot to corner the spit market.

·   ·   ·

Delay at TTC Pape station as 16 teenagers are entering puberty there this afternoon.

Just hiked up my pants. There's gotta be a better way to say this.

I'm open to citizens' suggestions of things to carp about. I'll be carping from 2-3 pm today anyway, so you might as well get in on it.

In my opinion, dusk is a little too fond of itself.

Hollywood's Walter Pidgeon in town today to have the 'd' removed.

Those dim Eaton brothers (Dinty, Thad, Syntax, Mo and Tab) are slumming it here at Fran's St. Clair. I sent a bottle of bleach to their table.

With midnight come the pigeons of doubt.

City Hall always looks lovely on a Saturday evening: it's emptied of people, so it's full of potential.

It must be admitted that we didn't foresee use of the Wychwood Park Aerial Tramway by immoral members of the 1/38th Mile-High Club.

In this city, the milk of human kindness has curdled.

Coming to the CNE Grandstand this summer: Morey Amsterdam's SEZ WHO?, with a galaxy of your favourite vaudeville stars, plus free tubs of white shoe polish.

. . .

A delay caused by a jar of spoiled mayonnaise thrown on the tracks is TTC emergency code #882, or, informally, an 'electric chicken'.

Five Detroit mobsters posing as CBC radio announcers to evade arrest were nabbed by police this morning. Dead giveaway: their diphthongs, dames and dental work.

Soup of the Day in Toronto today is: Hot Liquid.

This morning I'm guest-hosting CFRB Radio's phone-in show for the moist and talkative '*Say It, Don't Spray It*'.

Operators are not standing by. Be realistic.

Tonite on *MANNIX*: Joe suspects a computer dating company is matching people according to their needs rather than their wants.

City of Toronto's 'Spill Your Guts' phone line closed tonight to allow staff time to wolf down some pie.

Comedy-tragedy strikes at CNE as Embargo the Clown slips on a banana peel, but not one of his own.

Wayne Newton and the Boise Castrati Choir to light up the CNE Grandstand, and probably stink up the Food Building.

Threw my back out this week stabbing an alderman in the back.

I'm relaxing in the alcoholic pudding lounge atop the Bulova Tower whilst watching Russian sailors competitively piss into the lake.

· · ·

Two hours left to enjoy the Don't Deny It Toupée Bazaar at CNE Automotive Building -- thousands of rugs, lids, turf hats, skull fabric and he-wigs.

Delay at TTC Woodbine as we need to put the kibosh on the lowdown.

Fun Fact: there are 63 people in Toronto who only eat cotton candy.

To raise $$ for Ladies' Lukewarm Wading Pool, we'll issue municipal bonds payable in City Hall cafeteria sandwiches in the year 1997.

Toronto is in no way ready for topless and/or bottomless taverns. I suggest we start with nude hosiery and then assess.

I enjoy debris.

When I was a lad, no one could spell the word ukulele, and we got by just fine.

I shall NOT be attending the Projectionists' Picnic at Centre Island. It's a disgraceful priapic affair, involving hookers and silver nitrate.

CNE midway ride Blindfold Taunt is closed today for insurance reasons.

CNE Air Show highlight today: helicopters dumping unclaimed luggage into the lake.

CNE Food Building safety violations include cotton candy with actual cotton; triangular bagels; descrambled eggs; inedible panties.

. . .

Tonite at CNE Grandstand: music band 1910 Fruitgum Co. perform their hit song while surrounded by security guards born in 1910.

Your TTC transfer is valid on these CNE rides: Hav-A-Nap; Tumble Dry; Fainting Spell; Prickly Divorcee; Vomitorium.

Tonite at CNE Grandstand: Absorbine Jr. presents The Show Me Where It Hurts Show -- 150 out-of-shape men lifting heavy objects incorrectly.

Delay on TTC Yonge line as customized Manure Train carrying police horse droppings glides ominously from Union to Davisville.

Blown fuse at CNE Butter Sculpture Museum means John Diefenbaker and Charlton Heston now flow together in one melted river of rancidity.

Tonite at CNE Grandstand: The UnWelkome -- baritone singers booted off The Lawrence Welk Show for their socialist views.

At this time of nite, Fran's on St. Clair is full of the divorced, the disdained, the dissonant, Pomilot sauce and Glenn Gould.

I've lifted the city-wide xylophone ban, but don't make me come up there.

I've asked the Police Chief to round up the city's architects and deliver them to my office at 8 a.m. I want more Babylonian oomph!!

Toronto leads its latitude in moping.

· · ·

We're getting bids via Telex from as far as Macau and Mimico for surplus City statues of a tastefully nude Mary Pickford.

We have ponds in Toronto.

Opening Friday at the Imperial Six: the cutthroat world of the throat cut styptic pencil industry is exposed in Brian De Palma's *CLOT*.

Lucille Ball is peeling the wallpaper off here at the Royal York Imperial Room with her screeching rendition of the theme from *OUR MAN FLINT*.

Tonite on *MANNIX*: Joe nabs an art thief by posing nude at the Louvre and seeing who isn't interested.

The TTC delay you are currently experiencing is a different delay than the previous one, and yet they share so much in common.

Sunoco gas station at Bayview and Millwood out of gas, is now pumping out damned lies.

Traffic on Highway 400 backed up for miles as dozens of fathers insist on changing out of their flannel trousers and into their swim trunks on the highway.

Balliol St. closed tomorrow for mispronunciation.

Would the owner of a lime green hearse, with the licence plate 'ATTABOY', please drive it directly out of town.

· · ·

Typical Imperial Six afternoon: brassy dames ejected; bikers pinioned by ushers; complaint of brittle Twizzlers; boos for Karl Malden.

Peter Ustinov in town today to promote his *SPARTACUS* line of office thongs.

I have just been informed that the Bloor Viaduct is a drawbridge. So we could have been sailing galleons up the Don River this whole time.

Latest addition to this summer's CNE Grandstand shows line-up: 800 children compete in the Snitching Bee, hosted by James Mason.

If re-elected, I will raise taxes, but lower the lights to make the city sexier.

An election debate has been scheduled with my corpse-like opponents, rickshaw salesman Bub Erg; failed postal clerk Dennis Pinch; Mimico wigette Ina Pert.

Tonite on *BONANZA*: Hoss sees a woman for the first time.

Powerful Union of Toronto Building Lobby Security Guards is working to rule by only having visitors sign in, but NOT sign out.

I'm at a huge pothole on the Gardiner Expressway. It's like staring into the abyss, except this one has a burning Becker's milk truck in it.

Take it from me: never trust an archaeologist. They see everyone as potential loot.

. . .

I structure my days as per classic motion picture story arcs. Today's 'inciting incident' was an encounter with a rotten grapefruit.

Yorkville Ave. closed today for revamping. Previous vamping didn't work.

Please note: CNE Grandstand Show *KITTENS AND HAMMERSTEIN* — 300 cats hissing Broadway show-tunes — has been cancelled due to mange issues.

BREAKING: Pope Gerald II to land briefly in Toronto today to refuel his plane and to excommunicate Mr. Don Pea of 2043 Pape Ave.

Dufferin St. closed tonight to prevent people from going to Dufferin St.

Toronto restaurant reps beseeching me and City Council to allow them to glaze foods other than hams and doughnuts.

I've ordered police to jam the signal of Radio Free Coxwell, a notorious propaganda arm of greasy hippies seeking free patchouli.

Marxist-Leninist-Projectionist here has locked himself in booth, citing 'hegemony'. Smoking him out with 'Rockefeller' cologne fumes.

Fun Fact: all the ice in the Titanic iceberg could be distributed -- and melted -- in Toronto's urinals, with few deaths.

Toronto's last bespoke toilet plunger boutique, Shitstick's of Versailles, going out of business cause we can no longer have nice things.

. . .

Rogue's gallery closed today to add scoundrels.

In Victorian Toronto, the name 'Lloyd' had three L's, but the third one could be used anywhere in the spelling.

Tonite at the CNE Grandstand: Dick Van Dyke trips over the world's largest ottoman.

Egghead helmer Stanley Kubrick in town for his next impenetrable projectionist's nightmare, *THE PROJECTIONIST'S NIGHTMARE*, with Rip Torn.

23% of TTC passengers only take a transfer because of peer pressure.

City of Toronto Archives, Fonds 1244, Item 2046

"YOU SIR, YES YOU -- STEP INSIDE
AND MEET THE QUEEN BEE!!! SHE WILL POLLINATE YOU
WITH COURAGE AND VALOUR!!!"

"YOUR RATIONS WILL BE HONEY, YOUR PAY PACKETS
WILL OVERFLOW WITH THE STINGS OF VICTORY!!!"

My old man used to draw a crowd each year at the Canadian National
Exhibition with his crazed pleas for men to join his bee army.

14

THE ROAD TO RUIN, AND TO ETOBICOKE

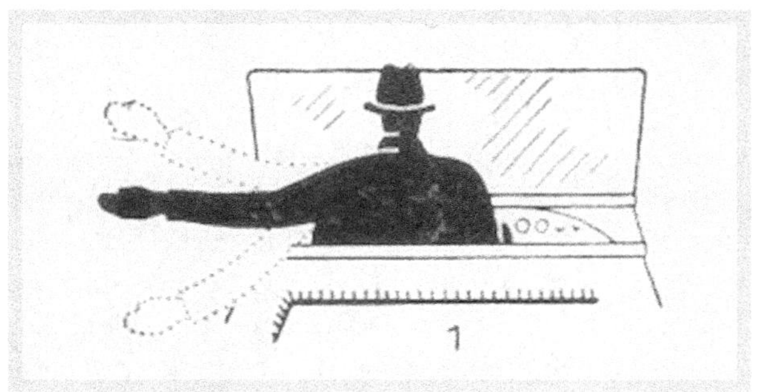

Legend has it that the shape of the Gardiner Expressway precisely mirrors a varicose vein on the leg of Fred Gardiner, its builder. I was omnipresent, and omniscient, at City Hall at the time, in the mid-1950s, though I never glimpsed Fred's naked flesh below the waist. But I can only thank heaven that the expressway wasn't inspired by the vein that bulged on his forehead when he was in an apocalyptic rage, as drivers would now be ending their commutes in international waters south of Centre Island.

I have little patience for those who now rail against this temple of tire marks, this edifice of en routed-ness, this plateau of pre-parking, for it is one of our city's most endearing and cuddly public works. Indeed, if not for the shortsightedness of dreary pedestrianuts and gormless politicians, the Gardiner Expressway's full glory would be ours to behold, and to be fiscally beholden to. Who amongst us has not dreamt of ascending to the sky, rising above the grime and the gum, to see the world as the gods must have done so (albeit gods satisfied with a modest height for their Olympian perches)?

And to sit astride a city, all the while ensconced in a 1963 Chevy Biscayne, a metallic-smelling breeze caressing your cheeks as Ritz Crackers, cheroots, and the latest issue of General Hooray, linger at your fingers. What else, other than democracy and fat-free salami, could one want? The Gardiner's sexy narrow-waisted design means that drivers progress at a speed that allows them to contemplate life in all its mystery: why am I here? Who is that idiot ahead of me? Oh, the humanity, etc.

In Fred Gardiner's original Speer-like vision, this expressway would have connected to 17 other new asphalt cousins, linking the far-flung wastelands of Leaside (via the Chick Chesterfield Parkway) to the denuded slush fields of Forest Hill (via the Lorne Greeneway), from the psychiatric wards of Willowdale (via the John Diefenbaker Becauseway) to the chipmunk-infested flea markets of Scarborough (via the Avro Arrow Aqueduct). The shade these crisscrossing aerial roadways would have provided to 83 per cent of Toronto might have kept our sun-shy Scottish citizens pale, but such is the price we pay for progress.

And while many gripe about the claustrophobic and clammy gloom beneath the Gardiner's mighty arches, they would do well to consider what economic engines were once planned for there, including the British Commonwealth's first drive-thru divorce court, high-speed grease traps, manslaughter morgues, and a student driver reform school. We can only dream of these now. Aeons from now, archaeologists in their platinum future pants will uncover the glory that was the Gardiner, and wonder to themselves, "How could they build something so exquisite, and then fail to finish it?"

City of Toronto Archives, Fond 1266, Item 11609

When I was a lad, this is how contentious political issues were settled in Toronto.

15

THE INTERNATIONAL HYPHEN ASSOCIATION

The star of CHICK CHESTERFIELD: TORONTO DICK (i.e., me)

Imperial Six is hiring! I need: Twizzler Repairman; Tony Curtis Look-A-Likes; Marquee Sign Pole Suction Cup Whisperer; Crowd Pleaser.

I'm pleased to announce the appointment of Toronto's first robot laureate. Selectro will count the number of broken fire hydrants, then muse about them.

. . .

Taxi service will be intermittent today, as drivers are required to report to City Hall for annual anecdote inspection.

I had at first thought that Eaton's was putting out Halloween merchandise a bit early this year, but it's just a sale of aldermen's death masks.

Always-on-the-go Captains of Industry appreciate the stark but sweet efficiency of Tony Ontario's Pie Crust Hob-Knobbery on Pape. No filling, just crust, and then on to those lucrative sludge and hairnet deals!!

An experimental Belgian Disco Ball Dirigible, aloft and forgotten by CNE Air Show officials, has deflated and is inelegantly draped across Highway 401.

Proudly opening the Yvonne De Carlo Reference Library. Every damn book ever written about this lovely lady -- and a few volumes that aren't!

Tonite on *MANNIX*: Joe's turtleneck sweater makes promises his corduroy slacks can't keep.

I'm meeting with top executives from Canadian Specific Ltd., who are considering opening a massive excuses factory here.

The tradition of washing your underpants in the Don River on Labour Day and drying them with a magnifying glass is no longer popular.

Tamblyn's Drugstore Blimp above Toronto is not part of the CNE Airshow -- it is spraying acne medicine over high schools.

. . .

Firefighters are too busy today to rescue kittens stuck in trees, so I'm sending out bookmobiles with yarn on their roofs.

Wildcat strike at Simcoe St. Goatworks now over. Chief union demand met: that workers be allowed to lie about where they work.

Know the sawdust school janitors toss on kids' barf? The City makes a pretty penny selling it to schools! Or so sez our Vomit Forestry Dept.

Eaton's vans packed with nuisance raccoons are now on their way to Oshawa doorsteps (tee hee!). We feed the lovable rascals Mars bars and lard on the way!

Finally, breakfast! But quack doctor has me on the Gent's spleen diet: corn husks, pomegranate poi, octopus suction cups, and pebbles. Bleh.

Sayvette's is offering 2-for-1 coupons for its signature Doppelgänger line of men's two-legged tear-away sexual intercourse pants.

Whether you cast your precious ballot for me or for my opponent, war profiteer and he of ghastly breath, Z. P. Wallaby, consider that *without* me Pape and Dufferin will run with pus, infants will wail for their own amusement, and the TTC will be a toy of the military.

Nightcaps last night with pals from the fumigation insurance industry. Lounge singer did Wilfrid Laurier impressions all night -- thin act.

Tonite on a very special episode of *TOUPÉE COP*: Bruno Gerussi has to gently break the news to a room full of bigwigs - - their lustrous toupées are phony, made from tarantula pubic hair.

· · ·

Council debating if Toronto should start its own manned space program. We've already got 1) diapers, and 2) a willingness not to shave.

On a scale from 1 to 10, I'm always going to be the guy who owns the scale.

President Nixon's plane is refueling at Malton today. I'll be there with a mound of Shopsy's corned beef and ribald anecdotes about Kirk Douglas for him.

Morey Amsterdam in town to auction off 800 jokes lacking punchlines.

Charles Bronson, Charlie Callas and Charles Nelson Reilly aren't gonna blink in contact lens heist pic *I KNOW IT'S HERE SOME-WHERE*. Opens Friday.

If men wore lipstick I bet there'd be a nice Hunter Green.

Toronto's Time Capsule District is booming! It's here where things are put inside other things, not to be seen for centuries.

TTC streetcars are backed up on Queen St., meaning we'll have to implement the emergency Conga Protocol.

Peter O'Toole in town today to stare off into the distance.

Sexual glutton Peter Lawford uncovers a criminal plot so devious it has its own librarian in *NOW IT'S YOUR INFARCTION*, at the Imperial Six.

.   .   .

New 'new car' smells for 1974 models: Burnt Warranty, Eau d'ometer, Liver and Bunions, Chanel No. 401, Yield Sweat, Love Department.

Tonite on *MANNIX*: after years of confusion, Joe finally 'gets' lint.

A pimply biologist (Charles Bronson) and a foul-mouthed helicopter pilot (Shelley Winters) can only find love when the tide is out, in *THE EELS OF YONDER*, opening Friday at the Imperial Six.

International Hyphen Association is meeting in Toronto this week, so our city is overrun with Johnny-come-latelys, ne'er-do-wells and inter-provincial nabobs.

University Ave. closed today as the hospitals air out their dirty laundry.

Opening Friday at the Imperial Six: you can kill a man just by massaging his ankle in a certain way, or at least that's Larry Hagman's theory in *FATALITY SCHOOL*.

When I was a lad in the 1920s, everyone fully expected that Toronto would not be necessary after 1935 or so.

I find fog to be sassy.

Opening at the Imperial Six: aspirin has never been funnier as Martin Balsam and Martin Landau rub each other's temples in *HEADACHE HOLIDAY*.

Milton Berle in town today at a cleavage convention.

.   .   .

So sunny! University Ave. is like the Champs-Élysées! Except in Toronto there are no champs, and nothing is ever élysées.

Shaming doesn't work, so the library is rolling out the Overdue Book-Mobile -- speed readers will finish the damn book out loud for you.

I'm compiling a list of things that are squeezable.

My sleeves are at half-staff today, to mourn the passing of the pre-Confederation work ethic.

In Victorian Toronto sawdust came in twelve flavours.

Many people are flocking to Toronto, despite our stern anti-flocking laws.

Closed today: seaweed auction houses; decoder ring repair kiosks; voodoo cinemas; brochure writer night schools.

Jarvis St. is like a man in a bathrobe wearing a tie -- we can see what you are trying to do, and it's not working.

My wolfhounds, Ossington and Islington, are out for a frolic. Sobering realization: their petrified feces mounds will outlast us all.

Leafs goalie Gus Lumberberry out for tonight's game due to an upper-body injury, which I'm told is the inability to tell the truth.

At the Likely Story Dinner Theatre "where implausible meets boil-able". Best to bring your own pats of butter, as there are refrigerator issues.

· · ·

Ladies have bridal registries, now gents can list wishes at City Hall's Groom Registry, which is just a list of men with wishes, but still.

Toronto's last dumbwaiter showroom, the Moveable Feat, is closing after 70 years of easing the delivery of rice pudding to despicable aunts.

You can cut the tension with a butter knife in Hitchcock's suspenseless clock-watcher *RUMINATE*, opening Friday at the Imperial Six.

In a cruel twist of fate, caramel is delicious.

Fun Fact: City of Toronto's orange parking cones are made by Don Jail inmates from the transcripts of their lies.

I'm fanticipating tonite's cabaret show by Efram Zimbalist Jr. at the Royal York: songs by singers under FBI surveillance.

Globules of fat oozing down Jarvis St. are a natural by-product of the socio-restauranto complex. Please swerve accordingly.

Opening Friday at the Imperial Six: Telly Savalas, Joey Bishop, Karl Malden and Captain Kangaroo in arthritic thriller *SIT THEY MUST*.

Heading to Leaside's reliably disreputable Passenger Pigeon Cabaret-Tavern on Laird. It's the place where your worries go extinct.

Put me down for one of the new motorized shoehorns -- with built-in heel detector that uses drugged centipedes -- now at Sayvette's.

· · ·

Tonite on The Ed Sullivan Show: Ed welcomes The Filing Wallendas, the less-adventurous members of that famous family.

Inspecting City of Toronto's new Men's Necktie Incinerator on Pape Ave. The many gravy stains add a sweet, sad tinge to the flames.

I just hung up on Raymond Burr. Feeding him his *IRONSIDE* dialogue by phone while he's shooting isn't worth the aggravation.

My Hollywood spies tell me Jim Nabors has signed to play Mafia hitman Dirk Placebo in Sam Peckinpah's *RUBOUT* in 1974.

Lee Marvin is at Sayvette's Thorncliffe today signing *DIRTY DOZEN*-themed Halloween costumes, "ideal for the child who doesn't wash".

Drop in soup sales blamed on the rise in popularity of Fu Manchu moustaches. Don't say I didn't warn you.

In Danish cinemas, the manager explains the plot of a film in advance to the audience, so they can focus on the acting.

The TTC will no longer issue free disposable paper pyjamas to riders on the Yonge St. night bus.

Desi Arnaz and Desi Arnaz Jr. are both in town today, but it's a coincidence as they aren't speaking to each other.

Mrs. Xanadu seems to be wearing that new perfume from the Etobicoke Wives' Union called 'Cold Shoulder '.

· · ·

Tonite on *KOJAK*: halfway through the episode it becomes apparent that that isn't a lollipop at the end of the stick.

Fun Fact: if all the old men in Toronto who enjoy coughing up phlegm were to do so simultaneously, you'd still ignore them.

Hosting man-nificent action hero Peter Lawford at Imperial Six. He's in town to cast a thug or thugette for his new internationally violent pic *TEX-MEXPLOSION*.

We now have a separate wicket at City Hall where the Unreasonable may present the Unfeasible.

Prehistoric cave drawings have been discovered in the Don Valley!! They seem to describe some primitive form of zoning.

Don't forget: for every Toronto seagull that's evacuated its bowels, there are another 1000 waiting for the right moment.

We're unable to quickly retrieve the 50,000 false eyelashes spilt in 401 accident, so I've ordered them blown away to adorn the sky with their beauty.

Sure signs summer in Toronto is over: the galoshes barges from Rochester have started arriving, and people have stopped reading novels, are now only reading obituaries.

Today's solar eclipse has been downgraded to a taupe cloud over Etobicoke.

I've just been thanked for doing a thankless job, which kind of takes the frisson away.

. . .

Police called to frenzy of savings.

One can tell autumn has arrived in Toronto by the muffled roar of tens of thousands of corduroy pant legs.

Anticipation is mounting, but unfortunately so are the chimps, at the official opening of Riverdale Zoo's Animal Husbandry Motel.

Pape St. closed tonight to allow Wayne and Shuster to film a series of Louis St. Laurent gags.

Fracas on Front St. as two taxi drivers argue over what's the most lucrative time-wasting route from Union Station to Royal York Hotel.

For your amusement, Imperial Six ushers will be re-enacting *THE GREAT ESCAPE* in the lower lobby tonite, but, for safety reasons, only the document forgery scenes with Donald Pleasance.

If Frank Lloyd Wright got a peek at Toronto's skyline today, he'd be rolling in his grave, except that his casket is vertical, and it leaks.

City of Toronto Archives, Fonds 1257, Series 1057, Item 4024

That's me, behind #61, with The Fighting Euphemisms, representing our very own Mt. Pleasant Cemetery High School. We made it all the way to the Catsup Cup that year, but just as Ontario Chief Undertakeress Mrs. Polly Din was hailing us, we had to leave to study for our grave-digging exam.

16

WHY CAN'T MEN BE BUXOM?

I t's now officially winter in Toronto: park gates have been welded shut, 3,000 tons of pre-emptive salt has been dumped on streets, Centre Island removed from maps.

Seasoned NHL watchers anticipate that the Leafs will have the edge tonight as the Miami Screaming Eagle's new flamingo-shaped skates are not aerodynamic.

Don't forget tomorrow night to switch to winter toilet plungers.

Heading to the Royal York for Lorne Greene's sullen *BONANZA*-themed musical revue *DESPONDEROSA*.

· · ·

I've never seen a man rely on a barrel and shoulder straps to hide his nudity, and yet it persists due to Hollywood union rules.

Tonite on *TOUPÉE COP*: Bruno Gerussi rediscovers the meaning of Christmas by tossing counterfeit toupées he has seized out the window of his car onto the bald or balding heads of sad passersby.

Some say change in Toronto happens at a glacial pace. But glaciers formed the Avenue Rd. hill, and as a result I've made some good apartment deals there.

Goatee curfew lifted.

Tonite on *MANNIX*: Joe misinterprets a shapely widow's forthright and unambiguous request for sexual intercourse as some sort of stock market tip.

Autumn leaves clogged her drains until HE fell into her bed. *MY EAVESTROUGH LOVER* with Joey Heatherton and Gert Frobe, at the Imperial Six.

Paul Lynde in town the week to tape his Christmas special, *SMIRKING TURKEY* at CFTO-TV, with guest stars astronaut Neil Armstrong and Charo.

Toronto's most enduring hermit, Gus 'Garbo' Flanagan, has come down from his perch high atop Maple Leaf Gardens' former pigeon abattoir for one reason only: to renew his 25-year hermit permit. He scrambles back up, unaware that his silence license is about to expire.

· · ·

BREAKING: Archeologists have uncovered a lost Toronto ravine!! It's just off the Danforth and may be Aztec or Mafia in origin.

Now playing at the Imperial Six: Helen Hayes, Gabby Hayes and Isaac Hayes in *PURPLE HAZE*.

Just in from the Toronto Stock Exchange: pound cake stocks up 73%.

City staff will be shaking trees today to speed up goddamn autumn.

Now hiring: Imperial Six requires an experienced cashier who won't scoff at middle-aged men who have a crush on Karen Black.

Tonite on *KOJAK*: a mob boss begs for mercy when Kojak plays the same Greek music over and over and over and over and over again.

The Imperial Six's strongest usher can bench-press all six 35mm cans of Erich von Stroheim's depressing classic *GREED*. Not that we are showing it.

Loving this candied herring lunch in the garment district at The Tasty Fabric. Crotch seamstresses here make top $$$ due to the intricate and embarrassing nature of their work.

Fun Fact: when you pull the cord to ring the bell on a TTC vehicle it releases a shpritz of lemon-lime in my office.

Opening today at the Imperial Six: James Mason, Marsha Mason and Mason Reese in handlebar moustache courtroom drama *IF YOU SPRAY SO*.

. . .

My goofy son Xavier Xanadu just dropped out of yet another concierge school in Gstaad to be an '8-Track Tape Mogul'! Hey, Rockefeller: Sayvette's is hiring!

Latest poll: Bert Xanadu 87%, Pinhead 4%, Drooling Idiot 3%, Chronic Bedwetter 2%, Shoplifting Mumbler 2%, Chinless Wonder 2%.

There is 8% more Raymond Burr today.

Tiny tunester and *BATTLE FOR THE PLANET OF THE APES* star Paul Williams' next ape-ish epic is the cerebral *GOVERNANCE ON THE PLANET OF THE APES.*

To Whom It May Concern: this doesn't concern you!!

Hen-pecked husbands can learn to grow a pair at the Dufferin St. Testosterone Collegiate, now offering middle-of-the-night courses.

I once karate-chopped my way out of Harrods during a dispute over cheese. It's quite a story! Actually, that's pretty much it.

Supping with wrestling giants Tiger Jeet Singh and Flying Fred Curry at Maple Leaf Gardens' Hot Stove Lounge. Ah jeez, Haystack Calhoun just ordered tripe.

I often stand at the top of Hogg's Hollow, gaze north, and ponder the unrealized human potential of North York. But it's not in my jurisdiction.

A mediocre city runs on frustration, Wite-Out® and gasoline. A great city runs on coffee, hydro-electric power and pluck.

· · ·

I have invited Gordon Willis, cinematographer on *THE GODFATHER*, to adjust the lighting on Toronto's 100,000 streetlights. Just imagine Spadina in chiaroscuro!

Hmm. Just learned that I might be the only man who fries his Salisbury Steak in cognac and Ritz crackers crumbs.

Tonite on *MANNIX*: Joe shares a secret about his heinie, but during a commercial, so it is not broadcast.

Ottomans and chesterfields put out for trash on your lawn must be accompanied by a side table and lamp to make the situation more convivial.

In the next issue of General Hooray we ask Yvonne De Carlo "why do you hate upholstery?"

Top men in Toronto's galoshes industry tell me this dry winter is killing sales, so they might eliminate hideous buckles, use of plural, etc.

Put down that cup of joe and ask yourself: what have I done to make Toronto more attractive to James Bond movie location scouts?

Imperial Six projectionist Bub Molten just saw his shadow, so expect six more weeks of Peter Lawford films being out of focus.

City of Toronto's 300 pg. Directory of Houses of Sexual Congress is for official reference only and will not be read to you over the phone.

· · ·

Dining, if you can call it that, at Tony Ontario's Chip Dippery. Offers all the dips: onion and French onion. Comes with a syringe.

I predict Chuvalo in 13 rounds, followed by prolonged negotiations, then cake at Fran's.

Fun Fact: all City of Toronto librarians are authorized to tell you the ending of any Arthur Hailey novel.

There are no tolls on the road to success. However, there are greasy hitchhikers with explicit anecdotes about their bunions.

Wax paper should make up its mind.

Delay on the TTC Yonge line is as was foretold in olden times.

I am a municipal tyrant. I harbour no ambitions to be a regional or national tyrant --- seems like a lot of work.

Eating soup reduces the chances of making eye contact, so I rely on it.

I'm shaving in the dark to memorize my profile.

Tonite on *MANNIX*: the knob has come off the TV, so there's no way to watch this episode.

We welcome to Toronto recent graduates of the Ajax One-Week Welding School, who are now freelance spot-welding any loose shards they see.

. . .

Attention motorists: parking is like standing, but you're not in the car. Standing is like idling, but with intent. Idling is like waiting.

My Hollywood spies tell me that Dom DeLuise routinely refuses to say if he is in favour of world peace.

Tonite on *MANNIX*: Joe spills the beans on an old army buddy who is now a counterfeiter, but comes to realize that his own worldview has been a false shell, built on lies.

Feasting on Swedish meatballs as Toronto Maple Leafs maim the Michigan Soothsayers. Borje Salming tells me no Swede has ever seen a meatball --- it's all a marketing scam.

Get your mind out of the gutter, and while you're at it, pick up those twigs and bring them to this weekend's City of Toronto Twig Swap and trade yours for snazzier models!

No one can explain to me why, but felt is inherently disturbing.

Sod is Earth's toupée.

I fear that Buckingham Palace is now only sending tertiary members of the royal family on official tours to Toronto. We dutifully welcome to our fair city the Baron of Beef, Lord Haw-Haw and Lady Foot Locker.

In deference to ladies with finer sensibilities, TTC Coxwell subway station will be renamed Protuberance A-OK.

Avidly man-ticipating a reunion tonite at Old Ed's with my Barbershop Octet pals from Mt. Pleasant Cemetery High, The Styptic

Pencils. All are garrulous fellows, except for Percy, who has grown acetylsalicylic in the intervening decades.

Soup of the Day in Toronto today is Hot Buttered Slush.

Traffic moving imperceptibly on the Michael Snow Parkway.

I was just a precocious lad in 1923, but I do remember that Sackville St. was not so much a 'street' as it was a mammoth sluice for the leavings of the Dominion Caterpillar and Centipede Crematorium that graced that precinct.

Having a plate of corned beef oatmeal, gravlax and Ex-Lax at Fran's on St. Clair. The din of the blue-rinse set gushing about Bob Goulet is driving me nuts.

In the 27 motion pictures I helmed, I played Chick Chesterfield as a lovable cad, catnip for the ladies. He was the hotel dick at the Leaside Waldorf-Castoria, and was paid in seductive glances.

Spending a dreadful night at the opera — *THE FLACCID MISER OF GUERNSEY* at the O'Keefe Centre. I get enough zaftig German women bellowing at me at the office.

Eastbound Queen streetcars short-turning at Broadview out of fear of the unknown.

Just opened a time capsule in foundation of three-year old Kresge's store on Pape. Contains a still edible cheese sandwich and a chipmunk skeleton.

. . .

I'm making balloon sculptures at Don Jail to relieve tedium for hardened cons. Top request? My plastic depiction of the death of General Wolfe.

I'm keynote speaker today at a Jello luncheon hosted by the Septic Tank Repair Guild's Ladies Auxiliary. My topic: 'Why Can't Men Be Buxom?'.

We've set up a fake detour at Yonge and Bloor so you can avoid people with long-winded stories.

Tonite on *MANNIX:* Joe spends the afternoon monogramming his handkerchiefs because the crime rate has plummeted recently.

Tonite's reunion at the Warwick Hotel of my 1929 graduating class from Mt. Pleasant Cemetery High includes a giant cake shaped like failure.

Toronto Island's Centreville bumper cars are being driven slowly, if aggressively, along QEW to Buffalo for annual World Bumper Car Convention and Anger Management Fair.

You can't get a decent denouement in this city.

Rosedale socialites braying about traffic on Hwy. 400 are being soothed by Ontario Provincial Police aerial drops of photos of dreamy Cesar Romero.

What I'm giving to Halloween trick or treaters: edible parking tickets, half-baked ideas, palatable truths, sour grapes, second bananas.

When I was a lad, every Christmas my old man would order our entire winter supply of Styrofoam all at once.

17

'JESUS H. CHRISTMAS, IT'S HOT IN HERE!!!'

Imperial Six projectionists can make excuses 24 times per second.

City Hall's advent calendars are being mailed to each household today. Behind each door is a municipal rebuke, e.g. your eavestroughs are hideous, and a piece of fabric from the Shroud of Governance. Features illustrations from Victorian Toronto crab-apple industry labour disputes.

I'll be reading bedtime stories to the crews at the Don Valley road salt camp this winter, starting tonight with Charles Darwin's *ON THE ORIGIN OF SPECIES*, to inject some humility into these salty bastards.

. . .

Opening Friday at the Imperial Six: Yul Brynner IS Oscar Wilde in *GUTTER BALL.*

Soup of the Day tomorrow in Toronto is Cream of Indecision.

Lorne Greene in town today to have his mukluks plucked.

Back by popular demand at the Imperial Six: Sam Peckinpah tells Christmas to shut the hell up in *TINSELECTOMY*, featuring Woody Strode and Dr. Joyce Brothers.

Santa Claus Parade re-routed slightly to pass offices of Bay St. Captains of Industry, to remind them how miserable they are.

Cleveland Barons are sluggish tonite against Leafs, as they are playing in their stocking feet - skates held up at the border in laces dispute.

TTC Queen streetcars will be joining in the fun at the Santa Claus Parade! Each will be shrouded in black, representing the Ghosts of Christmas Past (Short Turn).

All cities look gloomy in November, giving Toronto, if only briefly, a fighting chance.

When I need to stand up for hours at a public event, I rely on Confederation Bros. Erect Rods to support and enhance my weary torso.

Some flights to Toronto's Malton International Airport have been to diverted to Milton Intranational Aeroport due to hairsplitting.

. . .

Toronto's own l'il promotional iceberg in the harbour, the Canada Drytanic (rye + ginger ale + cough syrup), hasn't yet melted due to glaze of geese urine.

Joan Crawford flays a Buick with a bullwhip in Andy Warhol's head-scratcher *POINTLESS OLYMPICS*, opening Friday at the Imperial Six.

Many people drink to drown their sorrows. I, instead, teach my sorrows to swim, and then treat them to a post-swim cheesecake buffet.

In Hollywood, a 'Joey Bishop Sandwich' is a scene in which a talentless hack stands between two stars to better amortize the lighting costs.

Police called to TTC St. Patrick station, just to marvel at its cylindrical narcissism.

I've ordered all Don River gambling barges to shore until further notice while we investigate rumours of frippery and roulette hypnosis.

Sam Peckinpah in town, at my suggestion, to shoot his new G-rated thriller, *BRING ME THE SHOE OF TIMOTHY EATON.*

In Victorian Toronto, City employees were bribed with offers of husbandry, lard patents and whooping cough-themed sheet music.

To lighten the mood, we will put a barbershop quartet in each TTC bus, deliver a free hummingbird to each home, and subsidize pudding.

Service on TTC Yonge line delayed by a tangle of venetian blinds in front window of train.

Soup of the day in Toronto today is Frisked Turkey.

My Hollywood spies tell me 'gaffers' don't actually exist -- just another accounting scam by studio bosses.

Ryan O'Neal in town today to deck a guy.

Opening Friday at the Imperial Six: Eddie Albert and Ringo Starr aren't the men they used to pretend to be in *NAP NEEDERS*.

Soup of the Day in Toronto today is Corrugated Lizard.

I've ordered the Gardiner Expressway closed till 6 a.m. so we can all just get one goddamned minute of silence for chrissakes.

My Hollywood spies tell me Brando out, Earl Holliman in as Don Corleone in the 1974 *GODFATHER* sequel. Also, Tony Newley has been cast as younger brother Ron Corleone.

Tonite on *IRONSIDE*: Raymond Burr insists on wearing a fright wig, destroying any suspension of disbelief.

Police called to idle boast.

Delay at TTC King station as two Ernest Borgnine impersonators scuffle in a turf war.

. . .

Screen actors: in order to cry convincingly for a scene, think of your tear ducts as your bladder, and the dialogue as five gallons of Satan's urine.

When first negotiating with a Hollywood agent, break wind. They will respect and fear you for it. It's in their nature.

Opening tomorrow at the Imperial Six: Woody Allen, Woody Strode, Woody Woodpecker and Natalie Wood in *HAIRNET HULLABALOO*.

Toboggan Police reporting no incidents today except for one dad who is being a dick.

Noshing on Eggs Lenny: eggs from chickens descended from chickens owned by people mocked by Lenny Bruce.

Join me, won't you, this New Year's Eve for my Lint Roller Levee high atop the CNE Bulova Tower as we brush off 1973 and glad hand 1974. Entertainment includes Imperial Six ushers using grappling hooks to demonstrate how to lower a drunken patron from a balcony, and edible wind chimes.

Shelley Winters in town tonite to switch on the seasonal Pape Ave. atheism lights.

In winter months, Ontario Place is used as a kangaroo court by the Australian consulate.

In Victorian Toronto, tangerines were unavailable, so people just held oranges farther away.

Soup of the Day in Toronto today is Thankless Gazpacho.

. . .

Overly-dapper actor David Niven in town to promote his new line of men's cologne/smelling salts *ABDICATION*.

Awkward silence as I welcome to City Hall Davisville Avenue's famous Lumsden Quints (Zeb, Gus, Tod, Arlo and Tallulah), now 58 years old, narcoleptic, dandruffy and unemployed.

Shocking Hollywood news: Efram Zimbalist Jr. and Sammy Davis Jr. arrested for false advertising -- they weren't named after their fathers!

Upholstery, like chiropractic, is a profession doomed by its own sparse terminology to be forever marginal.

By virtue of an ancient municipal codicil, each Aldermen get 6 lbs. of municipal tinsel, 5 pints of City Hall cafeteria egg nog and a soggy piece of Fort York to use as firewood.

In the Winter 1973 'celebrity' edition of the Canadian Tire catalogue I'm the young buck posing in a snowmobiler's truss on pg. 189!

Also in Canadian Tire celebrity catalog: Lorne Greene gutting a fish, Elwood Glover spray-painting a hubcap, and Punch Imlach next to a fridge.

Our annual census of Toronto pork chops is voluntary, but c'mon.

Delay at TTC Bloor station due to widespread reluctance.

The City's new fleet of very tiny trucks will come by alternate Wednesdays to collect your discarded doll house furniture very quietly.

. . .

We'll be labeling some City Hall office doors in Latin only, to keep the idiots out and therefore increase productivity.

Attention men with untrimmed nostril hair: 93% of women are shorter than you.

Dandruff levels in the city today are approaching 'cloudy'.

Pierre Cardin in town to design Gardiner Expressway tollbooth attendants' uniforms. I'm thinking Busby Berkeley meets Soviet cosmonaut.

City of Toronto hockey rinks use pucks are made from compressed goose droppings, and made by men with suppressed feelings.

Some streets remains icy and dangerous as road salt crew stayed up late watching Lee Marvin in *CAT BALLOU* for only the millionth time.

Mrs. Xanadu and I will be at the prestigious croutoneers' table at the Royal York Imperial Room tonite for Ethel Merman's annual Christmas pageant of songs and sweat, *JESUS H. CHRISTMAS, IT'S HOT IN HERE!!!*

Due to the intense cold, brakes are weak on the TTC Dufferin bus today, so service will be faster than expected.

Only 37 men, led by Anthony Zerbe, have the balls to take on the 'dress code' system and its arbitrary 'rules' about central upper thigh exposure, in *CAVALCADE OF TESTICLES*, opening Friday at the Imperial Six.

· · ·

His historically persistent diarrhea is back, but that isn't going to stop Geoff from his dream of being the only one-man team in a four-man Olympic bobsled competition, in *BLEACHED LIGHTNING 3: IT'S ALL DOWNHILL FROM HERE*, opening today at the Imperial Six.

Join me at City Hall tomorrow for the Shoehorn Industry Job Fair. All the top companies will be there: Shoe Shiv Ltd., Foot Assault & Sons, Dr. Doldrum's Maître D'heel. It's said that shoehorn careers can lead to opportunities in shoelace law and bunion masseusery.

Soup of the Day in Toronto today is Bone of Contention.

Driver of TTC Dufferin bus is riding the brakes today due to a toe-tapping tune he can't get out of his head, possibly bySammy Davis Jr., we are awaiting confirmation.

I've triggered the rarely used Lee Marvin Protocol, under which City of Toronto police officers are to operate on the assumption that everyone is trying to pull a fast one.

A lovely afternoon at Park Plaza hotel bar ruined by Pierre Berton and Farley Mowat comparing penis sizes, and using swizzle sticks to do so.

Compromise reached in lawsuit between rival Toronto makers of 'World's Greatest Dad' and 'World's No. 1 Dad' mugs.

Toronto is hosting the World Brochure Association convention in 1974! Highlight is a $1 million platinum brochure, which is about itself.

Come tour the world's largest gingerbread house in Nathan Phillips Square! Three storeys of candied drywall, licorice furnaces and pudding eavestroughs.

. . .

Delving is not allowed in Toronto after 9pm and is generally discouraged at any time.

Fun Fact: there has never been a report of a Marlene Dietrich-shaped cloud appearing over Toronto.

I'm blessed with versatile facial muscles, which allow me to easily disguise my contempt for others.

Imperial Six ushers are given free carrots, so that they may better see, and stop, the filthy things some of you do when the lights go down.

No Toronto street has a hairpin turn, as its roads were designed by men who'd never seen a hairpin, or gotten close to a woman.

The gravel the City uses to fill potholes comes from the crushed pyramid ruins of RKO Pictures' failed 1931 epic *AZTEC ERECTIONS*. I won 'em at poker!

Visiting City Council today: delegation of observers from the International Observers Association.

Embroidery is its own worst defence.

There will be more free space in Toronto on this icy cold day, what with men's scrotums shrinking.

Elwood Glover has asked me to host a new talk show on CBLT-TV, *'Don't Bother Asking'*, in which I'd cut people off.

. . .

Toronto forecast: widespread settling for less by midnight.

A heavily-medicated funeral home director (Wayne Newton) falls in love with a foul-mouthed freelance gravedigger (Sandy Duncan) in the motion picture everyone is walking out of: *THE YEARNING URN*, opening Friday at the Imperial Six.

Degenerate Leaside Santa Claus Parade never fails to spoil the season. Santa is played by a bouncer from The Moody Pancreas tavern, reindeer are mangy racoons, 'elves' are strippers from Laird Lap-a-torium, and sleigh is a munitions factory septic truck.

Bay St. closed today from 11-3 for the Parade of Emotions.

18

DOES TORONTO EXIST? AND IF
SO, WHY?

City of Toronto Archives, Series 381, SD281_JB040_JJ094_C

T hey don't call them the bowels of the earth for nothing.

Our city's particular portion of the global bowel is located seventeen
stories below City Hall, an ancient archives of pre-Toronto that is so
foul in its Facts, so off-putting in the Historic Horrors it documents, so
twisted in its undermining of our pleasant Civic Myths, that it wears
its bowelesque nature honestly.

. . .

Only I, as your Mayor, and Thad Itchington, the City's Ur-Archivist and Warden of All the Swans, have keys to this vault of truth-terror. It contains, on parchment both fetid and lovely to touch, the true purpose of Toronto --- the dark secret as to why it exists at all. I feel I can share it with you now, as I say fort-nightly to Mrs. Xanadu, if you will but endure some context…

Urban citizens, mired as they are in the muck of their thoughts, and in actual muck, can take for granted the existence of their city, without considering it could just as easily be, say, a turnip patch, perhaps the world's largest. Nary a day went by, as I would amble down Yonge St., or an alternate Thursdays, up Yonge St., passing the potato chip advertising agencies, hairnet clubs, ukulele pawnshops, doorstop rental kiosks, bingo caller night schools and underwear incinerators that I wouldn't think "surely there was a better, more moral and productive use for this space?'

I speak not as a cornpone advocate of the bucolic village, the misty-eyed hamlet or the sexually repressed rural assemblage of 1-2 people per square mile, but as a lover of cities, and a lover in general. My enthusiasm for big cities (e.g. the ready access a city like Toronto offers one to sample 140 varieties of denture cream, show off garish cummerbunds or snub blowhards like Pierre Berton) leads me not to question their being, but to advocate for a deeper understanding of their origins and purpose. Only with knowledge of the urbanic past can we, as citizens and civic leaders build the city of tomorrow, using the taxes of tomorrow and the union agreements of yesteryear.

Let's take Paris, France, for example. Mostly thought of as home to world's finest lapels, lapins and inviting laps, it was first conceived of by a wealthy medieval baron merely as a source of raw materials for the manufacture and adornment of his many gaudy codpieces. But, with this codpiece compulsion came an array of craft guilds, crotch measurers, mud amelioration consultants, kooky French caterers and hangers-on, and hey presto, a city was born.

. . .

Or, in more recent times, the licentious and frequently driven-past city of Reno, Nevada was first constructed, mostly out of cardboard, as the set for the Eadweard Muybridge zoopraxiscope production of *HARKEN UNTO MY CUFFS*, a 19th century soft-pornographical head-scratcher. Its addled cast of actors lingered, as did their aromas, long after production ceased, and their presence spawned a dump, a pudding viaduct and a pet shop, three of the crucial building blocks of any city.

What of other great metropolises? From what dusty purpose did they spring? Miami? Intended to be the world's largest towel-drying tarmac. Barcelona? It was meant to be a farm used to develop onions that don't cause people to cry. Düsseldorf? Its intended destiny can be discerned from its very name, formed from the ancient Greek words 'dussel' for 'duffel', and 'dorf' for 'dorf'.

And, so, what of our own beloved Toronto? John Graves Simcoe, the city's founder and, if all had gone according to plan, its assassin, intended (according to a parchment document, written in his own cake-stained hand) for Toronto, then called York, to be completely denuded of its fertile soil.

Its fragrant mud would have been stripped from its innocent surface, and shipped back to Simcoe's native England where he planned to make a fortune supplying the then-burgeoning market in mud-based dandruff treatments, so beloved by the scrofulous aristocrats of the town of Budleigh Salterton, known then as the experimental shampoo capital of Devon. But his dastardly plans went awry, thanks to the dermatological innovations of the enlightened Head and Shoulders families. And in the centuries that followed, Toronto developed into the shredder of dreams we all are distractedly fond of.

And so, when we curse Toronto's persistent soup smell, its dingy Parcheesi parlours, its flame-sputtering escalators, and its general pastiness, we might be best advised to pause and consider the alternatives.

19

NOW AT THE IMPERIAL SIX:
'PYJAMAS SUBPOENA'

Cheapskate Harold Ballard now has the Leafs practising on ice on College St. formed by a broken water main.

Fun Fact: the Toronto telephone dial tone is generated by a tuning fork being gently prodded by a retired nun.

Hottest Boxing Day special: Eaton's Milady brand Recent Divorcee Privacy Shrouds, in Denial Pewter and My Version Of The Facts Charcoal, 83% off.

Delay at TTC Rosedale station as Mrs. Eaton's ladies-in-waiting adjust her hoop skirt and iron her bus transfer.

. . .

I'm the sole guest on Elwood Glover's *LUNCHEON DATE* program today, as we tackle the troubling rise in the use of ponchos in our city.

The following schools remain closed due to snow plough turf wars: Pope Gerald Multiplication Tables Prep School; Mt. Pleasant Cemetery High; William Lyon Mackenzie-William Lyon Mackenzie King Mature Student General Interest Night School; North By Northwestern Secondary School.

Tonite's Maple Leaf Gardens show, *DIRTY HARRY ON ICE*, starring Eddie Shack as Inspector Harry Callahan and Anthony Zerbe (on a toboggan) as SFPD Homicide Inspector Frank "Fatso" DiGiorgio, has been moved to Nathan Phillips Square due to overflowing toilets and indifference.

Everything is fine: reports of shouting and furniture breaking at Bulgarian consulate on Lansdowne Ave. is explained by the fact that it is simply their quaint custom.

Prepare to cheat your maker in thrillicious Thai spy pic (slightly dubbed into English) *THE SPONGE-BATH ACCELERATION*.

If it were up to me, we'd have a Canadian or two on the moon by 1974, and bring them back when I'm good and ready. That's leadership.

TTC Finch station closed for embarrassing personal reasons.

I've been called the 14th Beatle, but I don't know what that means.

Due to a clerical error, garbage picked up yesterday from houses on Heath St. yesterday instead of tomorrow will be returned to owners today.

. . .

Huge line-up at the Imperial six for Liza Minnelli-Joe Namath buddy cop comedy *COP A FEEL*. By definition, these people have not yet seen the movie.

I have secretly been wearing slim-fit hip-waders all day.

Personnel department drunks in Toronto now have their own resumé-themed bar, The Top O' The Pile, where they trade weaknesses.

As it must to all men, death came this week to TTC streetcar service until June's thaw. The streetcars, their Bakelite, cardboard, bamboo and candy interiors as fragile as a spurned lover's ego, are too delicate for our Plutonian winters and, perhaps, for this mean world at all.

Tonite on *MANNIX*: Joe investigates a crooked dry cleaner who's lining his pockets with other people's pockets.

In subtle narrative protest, Leafs fans throw on the ice a pair of plaid pants, an ironing board and dinner for two at Ed's Warehouse.

City work crews are dredging the Don River --- its muck will be used to build a monument to Toronto's history of make-work projects.

Trains at TTC Bloor station are in a holding pattern till a better class of passengers show up.

Seven-year-old boys who wish to flatten pennies under TTC trains are invited to mail them to me, and I will see to it.

Sean Connery in town today to squander his manhood.

· · ·

Lunch at my desk: three dead capons, decaffeinated gravlax, butter soup, Prussian potato salad, spamwiches, gum pie and a flagon of Tahiti Treat.

Tonite on *MANNIX*: Joe regrets going with the capri pants when he finds himself trying to blend in at a Mafia dinner.

I'm enduring the 'signature' Christmas drink at the Park Plaza's rooftop bar. Ink Nog is made from pulped copies of Pierre Berton's latest non-fiction sleeping pill, *LAKE SIMCOE WOODEN LEG LIMER-ICKS*. It tastes like the B.N.A. Act mixed with Thrill gum.

I shan't be attending the ghastly annual Christmas party put on by the Imperial Six projectionists, to be held amidst panoplies of vodka sausages, vats of hot buttered gum, and collections of lost pantyhose at the Ontario Censor Board's warehouse of deleted nude crotch shots.

In the final episode of Bruno Gerussi's *TOUPÉE COP* it's revealed that....*<u>Bruno has been wearing a toupeé the whole time!!!</u>*

In Victorian Toronto it was the custom to give homemade leg irons (made of old dentures and donkey ribcages) as Christmas gifts to friends to save them from having to purchase them at the Lady Simcoe Recalcitrant Debtor's Prison.

Crotchety initials hog and sleep-inducer J.R.R. Tolkien is in town to rummage thru Toronto graveyards in search of painful consonants.

Do you have room on top of your radiator? City of Toronto road workers have hundreds of sopping wet socks that need to be dried.

· · ·

Opening this Friday at the Imperial Six: Lorne Greene breaks up a plot to melt the Stanley Cup for a Satanic ritual in *WALKIE TALKIE HOCKEY*.

Snowflakes are indistinguishable from dandruff, unless you know the guy.

Visiting morose workers again at the Don Valley road salt camp. These men won't see an orange, a woman up close, or an episode of *BARNABY JONES* for months.

City Hall rink closed today due to excessive salchows.

Scientists have proven that there is no place on earth quieter than a closed dry cleaner's when you can see your own shirts thru the window.

Fun Fact: silent movies continued to be made in Toronto decades after talkies because no one here had much to say.

Tonite on *MANNIX*: Joe suspects his dentist is just in it for the money.

BREAKING: Dean Martin & Jerry Lewis broke up because of the ampersand.

When I was directing and starring in my *CHICK CHESTERFIELD: TORONTO DICK* pics in the 40s, I was the first to use margarine as a plot device.

Toronto leads the globe in second thoughts.

· · ·

Delegation here today from the U.N. to study just how little information one can put on a receipt and still have it be considered a receipt.

On Saturday nights, the Chief of Police disturbs me only if there has been a heist that holds strong narrative potential.

Most nations of the world have consulates in Toronto, except for Prussia, which is represented by rage.

BREAKING re: traffic jam on Bayview Extension: teams are racing to the scene and blame should be shifted by 10pm.

I've issued a city-wide Wet Paint notice.

Simcoe St. Goatworks is introducing Goat Nog this Christmas. You don't want to know where the nutmeg came from.

Lineup extends from Imperial Six box office down into St. Michael's Hospital emergency dept. for Peter Lawford thriller *PYJAMAS SUBPOENA*.

The city's puddles are nameless, but that doesn't mean we don't know where they are.

I often think of fabric.

We ask that men with five o'clock shadows not congregate after 5 pm.

Guinness Book of World Records people are in town to count Toronto's cloakrooms. Some are among the world's most doleful.

.   .   .

Leafs will have to tough it out tonite, as Eddie Shack is off sick with a throbbing blackhead, and Coach Imlach is fighting the Spanish Fly.

Today's Soup of the Day in Toronto is Carrot and Stick.

TTC has released its blizzard skidding bus schedule, e.g. Dufferin St. southbound buses expected to spin out of control at 5, 6 and 8 pm.

If you are factoring in the wind chill today, you've already lowered your sexual attractiveness.

TTC Dufferin is currently idling at College, but then aren't we all.

Padded envelopes seem like they are up to no good.

I'm splicing subliminal images of Ernest Borgnine into all kids' movies to remind them you don't have to be pretty to be successful.

Rod Steiger is in town to play Santa at Eaton's. He's a method actor, so he's gonna need a reason to give your kid anything.

At any given moment in Toronto, at least 300 chickens are unaccounted for.

Hmm. In the novelization of 007's *DIAMONDS ARE FOREVER* there's no reference to the toupée Sean Connery is wearing in the film.

Today's snow flurries are brought to you by Stool Pigeon Dandruff Cream --- the brand that "can't keep a secret".

. . .

Due to slipshod management, most of the animals at Riverdale Zoo hit puberty today at 3pm, so don't wear red if you're going.

Christmas is proving to be too much for the delicate Mrs. Xanadu — her entire 'turkey' is constructed from egg salad, and she has caramelized the tree.

Fun Fact: Guy Lombardo and His Royal Canadians aren't really royal --- and they frequently denounce the monarchy when drunk.

In Victorian Toronto, beads of sweat on one's nose were collected and saved as savoury Xmas treats from gruff but fair Brother Nostril.

Christmas and Peter Lawford go together like metallurgy and mime, but this year the dapper denouement-doer has outdone himself with his latest motion picture, in which he wipes out a dozen nog-addled hitmen in *TWELVE ASSASSINS A-BEING WITHOUT VITAL SIGNS*, at the Imperial Six.

Just in time for that surreptitiously provocative man on your Christmas list! Sayvette's is now carrying Raymond Burr's *PERRY MASON* codpieces, including the popular Approach The Bench, Point Of Order, and Hostile Witness models.

Vehicles ticketed and towed today: Mr. Elmer Fabdottir's 1937 Chrysler Gristle (bumper fungus), Mrs. Pertaining Kilgallen's 1971 Oldsmobile Abdicate (chauffeur spoor), and a truck owned by Coxwell Gum Holsters (an Anti-Christ bumper sticker).

In Victorian Toronto, as there was only one store, and all it sold was cow dye, people exchanged glances for Christmas.

. . .

Mrs. Xanadu and I are at Malton Airport's VIP Salisbury Steak lounge for our flight to Paraflorida via Air Simcoe's 'Lieutenant Governor' class, for a week of sun, sand, scenery, samovars, soap-on-a-rope, soliloquies, subtle disgust from waiters, stubbed testicles and sobbing.

Tomorrow's comeuppance has been postponed till 3 pm.

Joan Crawford and two of her look-a-likes in town today to cash a cheque.

City Hall is closing early today, as it seems no one knows how to shut off the floor polisher, or even wants to.

Tonite on *MANNIX*: in the spirit of the Christmas season, Joe replaces his brass knuckles with a gently-worn rubber hose.

Police called to just make it all go away.

In Victorian Toronto, slush was an aphrodisiac, but back then life was so awful that anything was an aphrodisiac.

The International Bureau of Dry Cleaners convention at Lord Simcoe Hotel has been cancelled because nothing was ready when they said it would be.

The French have a word for that feeling you get when you mentally undress Ed Sullivan, but they refuse to tell us what it is.

20

THE PALACE OF GUILTY
PLEASURES

TORONTO STAR ~ JULY, 2003

USHERS & USHERETTES
FULL & part-time. Apply in person,
Imperial Six, 263 Yonge St.

I was a teenage usher.

I don't think anyone is going to make a feature film, à la *FAST TIMES AT RIDGEMONT HIGH*, based on my early 1970s adventures at the somewhat-forgotten and largely underrated palace of guilty pleasures, Yonge St.'s Imperial Six. But if they did, it probably would be called *USHERETTES GALORE*, or *EXTREME USHER*, or even *MATINEE IDLE*. And it would be the kind of movie that probably would have played at the Imperial Six. The kind of movie that wouldn't even get made for the straight-to-video market today.

Thirty years ago, on Friday, June 29, 1973, at a time when Trudeau still ruled, Nixon still scowled and Gary Glitter, Donny Osmond and David Cassidy still had fans, the Imperial Six opened, something of a revolution in cinema-going in Toronto. For me, it was an introduction to downtown Toronto, to girls, and to the imperious power that accrues to a 16-year-old when you give him a red jacket and a bowtie. I learned how to boss around thirty other ushers, learned about movies, and met my future wife. All for $1.85 per hour.

For moviegoers, it was a tastefully garish retreat, a cornucopia of movies and films (there's a difference). It was a place where fedora-wearing salesmen cared not so much what was playing as what time it got out. It was a place where fading movie stars' films went to die. (Do you remember David Niven in *OLD DRACULA*? John Wayne in *MCQ*? Richard Burton in *THE KLANSMAN*?) It hosted the stars of the day…well, okay, stars like Stompin' Tom Connors (who had his wedding reception there), Walter Pidgeon, Dan Hill, Xaviera 'The Happy Hooker' Hollander, and almost, Linda Lovelace (to the eternal regret of a dozen ushers, she didn't show up for the opening night of her soft core epic *LINDA LOVELACE FOR PRESIDENT*).

It was a lot of fun. Neither one of the grand movie palaces of the pre-TV era (although it had been in its previous incarnation as the 3,200-seat Imperial), nor a megagigaplex of the postmodern era, the Imperial Six sat somewhere between the two. It still evoked the excitement and spectacle of going to the movies but was, perhaps, one of the first signs that moviegoing was being transformed: fewer theatres, with lots of screens. Tens of thousands of people streamed through its doors during a preview week, just to look around --- before any movies were screening.

Architect Mandel Sprachman kept some of the old elegance of its past as a gigantic live theatre, commissioning original art (hanging sculptures made from metal and found objects, and giant fibreglass figures kissing in the dark), exposed unseen elements of the building (two of the theatres were constructed in the backstage spaces) and saluted the heritage of the building with historical signage and a sensuously surrealistic mural.

For a movie buff, there was no better place to come of age than in the dark at the Imperial Six. Compared to multiplexes of today, the Imperial Six was a combination rococo opera house, Edward Hopper painting and high-tech arcade. Think *BLADE RUNNER* meets Radio City Music Hall.

It lasted only 13 years before being transformed yet again, as a result of a bizarre real estate dispute. In its glory years, it was under the command of Phil Traynor, a formidable manager whose presence evoked fear in any ushers who dared to goof off, but who stood for the old picture palace values of customer service and showmanship.

Come Saturday night at six, Phil would appear on the balustrade overlooking the lower lobby, clad in a tuxedo and wielding a cigar of cinematic proportions. Think about it: When was the last time you saw an adult employee of a cinema, much less one wearing a tuxedo? For Phil, the cinema was his ship, and he was the captain, the 110 (!!) staff his crew, and the regular customers people he knew by name, and whose problems he sometimes helped solve.

Among them were the travelling salesmen, for whom the early matinees were welcome retreats from their Willy Loman treks. Phil recalls the line-up at the pay-phones when the first shows got out -- salesmen calling the home office to let them know they'd just gotten out of a 'meeting', when they'd really been watching *WALKING TALL* in Theatre 4.

The Imperial was one of the most profitable theatres in the Famous Players chain, and one that probably earned that status because its programming was deliberately broad, from the Gallic silliness of *THE TALL BLOND MAN WITH ONE BLACK SHOE* to the political thrills of *THREE DAYS OF THE CONDOR* to the kung fu mayhem of *SACRED KNIVES OF VENGEANCE*. The 1970s offered an eclectic and exciting range of films, with Scorsese, Coppola, Spielberg, Altman and many others redefining what was commercial, and the Imperial Six reflected that eclecticism.

It also was something of a haven for Canadian films, which struggled then as they do now for audiences. Films like *RECOMMENDATION*

FOR MERCY (about the infamous conviction of Stephen Truscott for murder) and *BLACK CHRISTMAS* (the Margot Kidder slasher flick) and *THE HARD PART BEGINS*, a story of a fading country music singer journeying through the small-town Ontario bar circuit.

On opening week, the Imperial Six presented a slew of white trash, disaster and Blaxploitation films, with a solid drama thrown in. *THE NEPTUNE FACTOR* was a Canadian-funded *POSEIDON ADVENTURE* knockoff with Ernest Borgnine; Robert Aldrich's *EMPEROR OF THE NORTH* pitted Borgnine against Lee Marvin (Borgnine on two screens! That's the kind of entertainment you don't get these days!); *THE HARRAD EXPERIMENT*, about college sex, was vigilantly checked by the ushers every several minutes; *DILLINGER* starred Warren Oates in a story told once too often; *THE FRIENDS OF EDDIE COYLE* was an edgy and underrated crime piece with Robert Mitchum; and *SHAFT IN AFRICA* was the second sequel to *SHAFT*.

As a young film enthusiast, soon to enter film studies at York University and twenty years later to produce documentaries at the National Film Board of Canada, the Imperial Six was a place to immerse myself in some of the best - *CHINATOWN, THE GODFATHER PART II, LAST TANGO IN PARIS* (Marlon Brando in the nude!) - and some of the weirdest - *FISTS OF FURY, MAGNUM FORCE, ZARDOZ* (Sean Connery in a thong!). I tried to learn from them all.

Despite the hype these days when *HULK or THE MATRIX RELOADED* open, there really isn't the same sense of event as there was back then. When was the last time you saw a line-up snaking down the block outside a cinema? But lining up carried with it a sense of anticipation, of privilege ('I got here first!'), and of a movie-going community (just ask the people in line at the Toronto International Film Festival).

The block from the newly-rejuvenated Dundas Square to Shuter St., as well as much of a stretch of Victoria St. at the cinema's back entrance, was jammed most Saturday nights as people jostled to get in to see *THE LONGEST YARD*, *WESTWORLD* (Yul Brynner as a robot cowboy) or *SERPICO*.

Remember movie marquees? There are a few left, but back then some theatres, including the Imperial, boasted of several marquees (we had two on Yonge St., one on Victoria), the curse of weak-armed ushers on a rainy Thursday night as they struggled with 15-foot suction cup poles to assemble the new line up in six cinemas, letter by letter. Occasionally, adolescent humour ruled -- for several hours one night, the Billy Dee Williams classic *HIT!* was adorned with the unapproved prefix 'S'.

It's hardly the only Toronto cinema of that era we have lost, and even if we don't mourn them all, hours spent in the 99 Cent Roxy, the Donlands, the Coronet, the Rio, the Fairlawn, the TD Cinema, the Towne, Cinecity, the Glendale and (sigh) the University were hours fondly blown. The Imperial and its ilk were the last cinemas opened before the two major 1970s movie revolutions: Home video, and JAWS-like megaflicks. Some of the D-movies moved out of the cinemas and into the VHS and Betamax machines. And why bother dedicating a screen or two to *NIGHTMARE HONEYMOON* or *THE ANTICHRIST* when you can squeeze some more profit out of *SPIDER-MAN?*

But the Imperial Six might have lasted some years more, if it hadn't been for a disagreement between Famous Players and the owner of part of the property, which brought an end to the era of bell-bottomed film exhibition…

Now the elegant Canon Theatre, home to live productions such as *THE PHANTOM OF THE OPERA*, and, this fall, *CHICAGO*, the building reveals none of its shaggy and sexy 1970's life. As for me, I can still find my way around in the dark without a flashlight. Blame it on the Imperial Six.

Gerry Flahive

AFTERWORD &
ACKNOWLEDGMENTS

Danny Flahive, TTC 'emergency man'

In 2009, I started pretending I was the Mayor of Toronto.

Long before Rob Ford, Mayor Bert Xanadu, a fictional civic leader, and owner/manager of the infamous and glamorously unlikely Imperial Six cinema on Yonge St., became my alter-ego on Twitter, as @MovieMayor.

More than 9,000 tweets later, I can declare that few things in my creative life have been as much fun and weighted with as little responsibility.

I was able, one tweet at a time, to build a familiar but, I hope, sweetly weird Toronto of 1973, with such area landmarks as the Simcoe St. Goatworks, the ghastly Slushfields of Oshawa, and Tony Ontario's Are You Going To Finish That? Restaurantorium, visiting stars like Morey Amsterdam, Joey Heatherton and ultimate action hero Peter Lawford (sic), and recurring heavily discounted sales at Sayvette's of Raymond Burr-themed pyjamas.

Bert is a heroic but delusional mayor, re-elected 27 times (Toronto used to have one-year terms for City Council), and whose favourite pastimes include re-zoning and giving speeches like 'Rubble: The Bastard Son Your Industry Needs to Acknowledge'. His equally important role as czar of the city's most velvety-red cinema allowed me to invent dozens of films that never played there, as they didn't exist, although they certainly should have, including *SEVEN APPEN-DECTOMIES FOR SEVEN BROTHERS-IN-LAW* and *MAIL-ORDER TOUPÉE HUSBAND*.

Bert's Toronto bears some resemblance to the Toronto I first encountered at the Imperial Six as a 16-year old usher, getting in fistfights with unruly patrons and organizing block-long line-ups for *THE TOWERING INFERNO* and *THE BEST OF THE NEW YORK EROTIC FILM FESTIVAL*.

*Me, out of uniform but full of attitude, in the Imperial Six ushers'
'lounge', circa 1974*

It was then that I truly discovered the downtown — swiftly modernizing, both socially and architecturally — that I'd barely glimpsed while obsessively touring 'new' City Hall on my own from about age 9, and learning the mysteries of the subway from my TTC mechanic dad, Danny, the 'emergency man' (remember '99 CALL CONTROL' over the subway P.A. system? They were calling him).

The Imperial Six feels now like a lovable and garish marker between two eras of show business, with elements of the old timey 'showmen' motion picture exhibitors who still lingered back then, and signs of the corporate multiplex approach to movie-going that was to come.

I had been using Twitter (as myself, @gflahive) in the early days of its existence as an occasional platform to invent fake Toronto International Film Festival parties (e.g., me hanging out with Klaus Kinski at Quizno's), which caught the eye of journalist Marc Weisblott, who started running them in his blog, Mondoville. When the festival wrapped up that year, he invited me to continue tweeting… something, and so I decided to combine two of my loves -- cities and movies -- and created Mayor Bert Xanadu.

(At first, he was Bert Wemp, the real name of Toronto's 1930 mayor --- and to confuse matters, I used a photo of a different mayor, Ralph Day, as Bert's avatar. A very nice man, Bruce Skeaff, Wemp's grandson, gently chided me for absconding with Wemp's identity, and so the Xanadu surname was born).

Bert Xanadu's very name was a combination of the mundane and the show-bizzy exotica that I imagined Toronto to exude. Bert (in my mind) was born in 1911, and so also carried with him all of the misplaced Anglo-Canadian smugness that often still holds Toronto back.

When the limits of Twitter started to chafe, I was able to write full-blown essays as Bert, and publish them with the connivance of Spacing's Matt Blackett and Shawn Micallef, and Torontoist's David Hains.

Many of Bert's tweets were super-powered by photos from the remarkable collection of one of our national treasures, the City of Toronto Archives. Given that I would often airlift their photos from their Twitter feed and then irresponsibly repurpose them only minutes after they had been posted, I must gratefully acknowledge the Archives staff for being such good sports, especially Archivist Paul Gardiner, who has been of immense help in scouring their collection for me. My apologies to the actual historical personages in the photos, whose identities I have scrambled.

As a respectable civil servant, i.e., a producer at the National Film Board of Canada, I kept my secret identity secret until I left the NFB in 2014, and I want to extend my thanks to those conspirators who kept it that way in those early years, especially Eric Veillette (who, as former manager of the beloved Revue Cinema, is the most likely successor to Bert Xanadu), Jonathan Goldsbie, Jennifer Mair, Grant McCracken and Melissa Than. Thanks too to David Battistella, Anne Brodie, Colin Brunton, Richard Crouse, Claire Dunn, Chris Frey, Michael Fukushima, Marc Glassman, Jeremy Katz, Angel Narick, Rama Rau, Elizabeth Klinck, Michael Redhill, Dylan Reibling, Ann Shin, Wendy Tilby, and Hawksely Workman, some of whom lent a kind eye to early versions of this manuscript.

Extra-Special Capitalized Thanks to artist Trevor Twells for his wonderful cover design.

Many thanks also to the mini-legion of Bert supporters, all now bene-fiting from preferential re-zoning of their City of Toronto properties, including Brent Butt, B.J. Del Conte, Ed Drass, John Fitzgerald, Jesse Hawken, Jerry Kitich, Jill Lum, Heather Mallick, Paul Moore, Pete Mosley and George Wolff.

Finally, my love and thanks to my wife Audrey McDonald and our daughters, Alice and Grace. They are too kind to tell me that I'm more like Bert Xanadu than I'm willing to admit.

ABOUT THE AUTHOR

Gerry Flahive is a writer and creative consultant in Toronto. He has been a frequent contributor to the Globe and Mail, and his articles have also been published in Time, The New York Times, the Toronto Star, The Times, the Los Angeles Times, the International Herald Tribune, the National Post, Spacing.ca, Huffington Post, MaRS Magazine, POV Magazine and The Walrus. He is a National Magazine Award humour nominee.

Until 2014, Flahive was Senior Producer at the National Film Board of Canada, which he joined in 1981. His documentary productions have won many international prizes, including two Emmy Awards, a World Press Photo Award, a Peabody Award and seven Canadian Screen Awards.